LEARN and USE English in Context

活學活用英文詞彙大圖典（修訂版）

By Elaine Tin

新雅文化事業有限公司
www.sunya.com.hk

A guide for parents 給父母的話

　　這本書適合從幼稚園步入小學，或希望打好小學英文基礎的孩子。英文千變萬化，單靠積累詞彙並不足夠。這本書除了擴充孩子的詞彙量外，還透過各種語境的例句、文法要點、親子對答和書末的 5 個對話活動，引導他們在日常口語中應用這些詞彙，逐步提升英文能力！

Themes 主題
透過 51 個跟孩子生活息息相關的情境主題，解釋各英文字詞的意思。

Let's Talk
家長可以跟孩子一起看圖學詞彙，一邊提問這部分的問題，讓他們應用所學字詞。提供的答案只供參考，孩子可自由回答。

Daily English
這部分的內容包括一些英語口語的慣用句式或特別說法，能幫助孩子說出地道英語。

Rules to Know
這部分以英文字詞為基礎，介紹一些簡單的英文文法規則，幫助孩子在認識字詞時自然地理解運用的方式。

Supermarket　超級市場

toiletries (n.) 洗漱用品
dairy product (n.) 奶類製品
bakery product (n.) 烘焙食品
tin and can (n.) 罐頭食品
household product (n.) 家居用品
shopping basket (n.) 購物籃
frozen food (n.) 冷藏食品
seafood (n.) 海鮮
meat (n.) 肉類
aisle (n.) 通道
produce (n.) 農產品
cart (n.) 手推車
rice (n.) 米
noodles (n.) 麵條
checkstand (n.) 收銀櫃枱
cashier (n.) 收銀員
self-checkout counter (n.) 自動收銀櫃枱
cash register (n.) 收銀機
sauce (n.) 醬料
confectionery (n.) 甜點
give change 找續 (找錢)
beverage (n.) 飲品
snack and nuts (n.) 零食和果仁
customer (n.) 顧客
pack (v.) 包裝
46　　47

Let's Talk
Q: Where can you find the bread?
A: I can find the bread in the bakery section.
Q: What do you usually buy at the supermarket?
A: I usually buy cheese and milk.

Daily English
到超級市場購買食物和日用品一般叫 do grocery shopping，又可以說 buy groceries。

Rules to Know
我們通常會在超級市場裏買很多東西，這時可用 a lot of 來表示「很多」，例如：
• I want to buy a lot of bananas.
　我想買很多香蕉。
• We need a lot of meat.
　我們需要很多肉。

Fun Corner
在超級市場裏的手推車除了叫 cart 外，還可以叫 trolley。

括號內的字為普通話用語。

Fun Corner
這部分提供一些與主題相關的額外英文知識，讓孩子體會英文的趣味！

這本書包含超過 1,600 個小學階段必學的英文字詞（words），不僅詞彙量豐富，而且都是生活中常見的事物，可以活學活用。

書中還有各種各樣的字詞，會在括號內標示詞性（part of speech），包括名詞（n.）、動詞（v.）和形容詞（adj.）。如孩子的英文程度高，家長可跟他們說明每個字詞的不同作用。

noun (n.) 名詞	We use nouns to name people and things. 我們用名詞來稱呼人物或事物。
verb (v.) 動詞	We use verbs to show actions. 我們用動詞來說明各種動作。
adjective (adj.) 形容詞	We use adjectives to describe how things are like. 我們用形容詞來描述各種事物的特點。

　　英文中還有其他詞性，例如副詞（adv.）和介詞（prep.）也會在書內其他內容中說明。

如何聆聽這本書的內容？

方法一 使用新雅點讀筆，點讀書中的字詞和四大欄目的內容（語言包括：英語、粵語和普通話）。

新雅・點讀樂園 升級功能

讓孩子學習更輕鬆愉快！

本系列屬「新雅點讀樂園」產品之一，若配備新雅點讀筆，孩子可以點讀字詞和四大欄目（Let's Talk、Daily English、Rules to Know、Fun Corner）的內容，聆聽英語和粵語，或是英語和普通話的發音。

想了解更多「新雅點讀樂園」產品，請瀏覽新雅網頁(www.sunya.com.hk)或掃描右邊的QR code進入 新雅・點讀樂園。

如何使用新雅點讀筆閱讀本書？

1. 下載本書的點讀筆檔案

1 瀏覽新雅網頁(www.sunya.com.hk) 或掃描右邊的QR code 進入 新雅・點讀樂園。
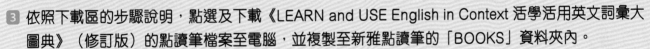

2 點選 下載點讀筆檔案 ▶ 。

3 依照下載區的步驟說明，點選及下載《LEARN and USE English in Context 活學活用英文詞彙大圖典》（修訂版）的點讀筆檔案至電腦，並複製至新雅點讀筆的「BOOKS」資料夾內。

2. 啟動點讀功能

開啟點讀筆後，請點選封面右上角的 圖示，然後便可翻開書本，點選書本上51個情景主題和插圖，點讀筆便會播放相應的內容。

3. 選擇語言

如想切換播放語言，請點選內頁主題右邊的 ENG×粵語 ENG×普通話 圖示，當再次點選內頁時，點讀筆便會使用所選的語言播放點選的內容。

方法二 掃描右邊的 QR code，也可以聆聽書中的英文字詞、欄目 Let's Talk 和 Daily English 的英文內容，學習發音。

Contents 目錄

Bathroom 浴室

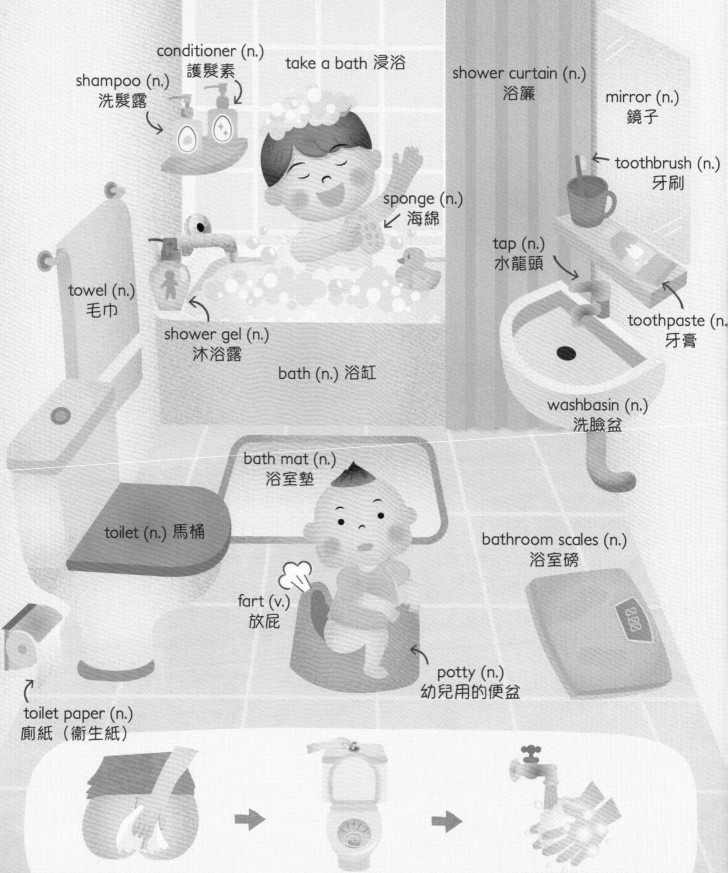

shampoo (n.) 洗髮露

conditioner (n.) 護髮素

take a bath 浸浴

shower curtain (n.) 浴簾

mirror (n.) 鏡子

toothbrush (n.) 牙刷

sponge (n.) 海綿

tap (n.) 水龍頭

toothpaste (n.) 牙膏

towel (n.) 毛巾

shower gel (n.) 沐浴露

bath (n.) 浴缸

washbasin (n.) 洗臉盆

bath mat (n.) 浴室墊

toilet (n.) 馬桶

bathroom scales (n.) 浴室磅

fart (v.) 放屁

potty (n.) 幼兒用的便盆

toilet paper (n.) 廁紙（衛生紙）

wipe one's bottom 擦屁股 → flush the toilet 沖廁所 → wash one's hands 洗手

take a shower
淋浴

showerhead (n.)
花灑頭

soap (n.)
肥皂

soap dish (n.)
肥皂碟

shower (n.)
淋浴間

wash one's face
洗臉

comb one's hair
梳理頭髮

hairdryer (n.)
吹風機

blow-dry one's hair
吹乾頭髮

squeeze the toothpaste
擠牙膏

brush one's teeth 刷牙

rinse one's mouth 漱口

Let's Talk

Q: How often do you brush your teeth?

A: I brush my teeth twice a day.

Q: When do you usually take your shower?

A: I usually take my shower before I go to sleep.

Daily English

當我們想上廁所時，要記得在不同的場合，會有不同的説法啊！

• 在公眾場所時，我們可以説：
May I use the washroom / toilet?

• 在家裏，我們就可以説：
Mom, I want to pee / poo now.

Rules to Know

我們每天都會在浴室裏做很多不同的事情，例如：wash our face（洗臉），brush our teeth（刷牙）。wash 和 brush 這些表示動作的詞語稱為動詞。

Fun Corner

Tissue 指放在口袋裏的紙巾，或是盒裝的面紙；toilet paper 則是卷裝的廁紙（衛生紙）。大家要分清楚啊！

7

Bedroom 睡房（卧室）

ENG × 粵語　ENG × 普通話

bunk bed (n.)
雙層牀

dresser (n.)
梳妝枱

lullaby (n.)
搖籃曲

crib (n.) 嬰兒牀

make the bed
收拾牀鋪

mattress (n.)
牀褥

bedsheet (n.) 牀單

wardrobe (n.)
衣櫃

bookcase (n.) 書櫃

Good night!
晚安

lamp (n.)
燈

quilt (n.) 被子

slippers (n.) 拖鞋

sleep (v.) 睡覺 / nap (v.) 小睡

snore (v.)
打鼾

dream (v.) 做夢

8

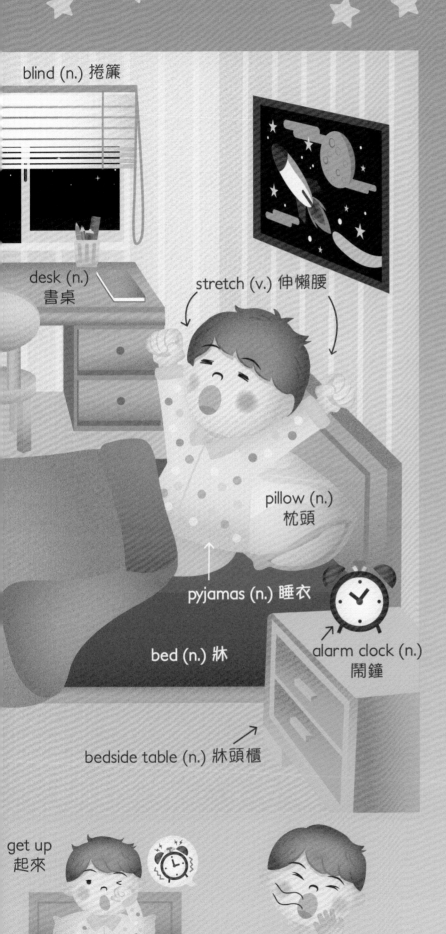

blind (n.) 捲簾

desk (n.) 書桌

stretch (v.) 伸懶腰

pillow (n.) 枕頭

pyjamas (n.) 睡衣

bed (n.) 牀

alarm clock (n.) 鬧鐘

bedside table (n.) 牀頭櫃

get up 起來

yawn (v.) 打哈欠

Let's Talk

Q: What do you see in this bedroom?

A: I see a little boy / some books...

Q: What do you like doing before you go to bed?

A: I like reading before I go to bed.

Daily English

除了 Good night 外，我們還可以這樣説晚安：
- Sleep tight!
- Sleep well!
- Sweet dreams!
- Nighty night!

Rules to Know

有些跟睡覺有關的詞語既是動詞，又能表示事物的名稱，叫做名詞。例如：

dream

動詞：What did you dream about?（做夢）

名詞：I had a nice dream last night.（夢）

Fun Corner

We have already put this issue to bed. 並不是指把問題放在牀上，而是表示解決了問題啊！

9

Living room 客廳

clock (n.) 時鐘

curtain (n.) 窗簾

television (n.) 電視機

dust (v.) 掃塵

window (n.) 窗

iron (n.) 熨斗
(v.) 熨衣服

monthly calendar (n.) 月曆

TV cabinet (n.) 電視櫃

coffee table (n.) 茶几

doormat (n.) 門墊

vacuum (v.) 吸塵

vacuum cleaner (n.) 吸塵機

household chores 家務

fold (v.)
摺 [衣服]

bucket (n.) 桶

mop (n.) 拖把
(v.) 抹地

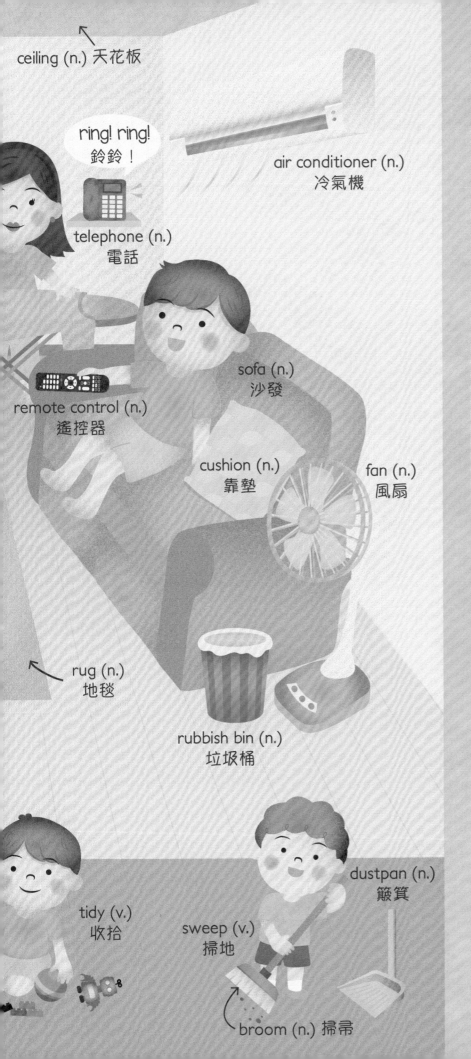

ceiling (n.) 天花板

ring! ring!
鈴鈴！

telephone (n.)
電話

air conditioner (n.)
冷氣機

remote control (n.)
遙控器

sofa (n.)
沙發

cushion (n.)
靠墊

fan (n.)
風扇

rug (n.)
地毯

rubbish bin (n.)
垃圾桶

tidy (v.)
收拾

sweep (v.)
掃地

dustpan (n.)
簸箕

broom (n.) 掃帚

Let's Talk

Q: What is the little boy doing?

A: The little boy is watching television / TV.

Q: What chores do you do at home?

A: I sweep the floor. / I take out the rubbish.

Daily English

我們常常在客廳裏看電視，如果想知道電視播放什麼節目，可以這樣問：

• What's on TV tonight?

• What's on Channel 2 today?

Rules to Know

在客廳裏，爸爸和媽媽都在做家務。我們可以用人稱代名詞來代指爸爸媽媽，說出他們在做什麼家務。

• Mom is ironing the clothes. She is very good at it.

• Dad is vacuuming. He likes to keep the house clean.

Fun Corner

中文「沙發」一詞是由英文 sofa 的發音而來。Sofa 是英式英文，在美國叫作 couch。

Dining room 飯廳

breakfast (n.) 早餐

cup (n.) 杯子
saucer (n.) 茶碟
teapot (n.) 茶壺

lunch (n.) 午餐

napkin (n.) 餐巾
drink (v.) 喝
lunchbox (n.) 午餐盒

dinner (n.) 晚餐

plate (n.) 碟子
mug (n.) 大杯子

picky eating 偏食情況

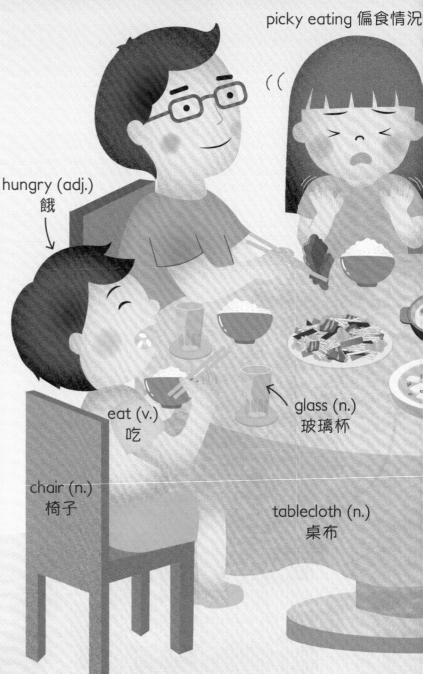

hungry (adj.) 餓
eat (v.) 吃
glass (n.) 玻璃杯
chair (n.) 椅子
tablecloth (n.) 桌布

set the table 擺餐具

place mat (n.) 餐墊

cutlery (n.) 餐具

Chinese spoon (n.)
中式勺子

sit at the dining table
坐在餐桌旁

g (n.)
水瓶

feed (v.)
餵

bowl (n.)
碗

coaster (n.)
杯墊

bib (n.)
口水肩（圍嘴兒）

high chair (n.)
嬰兒用的高腳椅

dry pet food
寵物乾糧

chopsticks (n.)
筷子

knife (n.)
刀

spoon (n.)
勺子

fork (n.)
叉子

Let's Talk

Q: What can you see on the dining table ?

A: I can see cutlery.

Q: How many meals do you have a day ?

A: I usually have three meals a day.

Daily English

當我們吃飽了，就可以說：
I am done.
如果還吃不夠，想多吃一點，就可以說：
Can I have some more, please ?

Rules to Know

飯廳裏的餐具常常可以用來表示食物的分量，例如：
• a glass of water　一杯水
• a bowl of rice　　一碗飯

Fun Corner

Dinner 是一天之中最豐富的一餐，因此我們一般用來指晚餐，隆重的晚宴也稱為 dinner。而 supper 可以指夜宵或晚上吃的那一餐，不過分量較少，吃的東西較簡單。

13

Kitchen 廚房

 ENG × 粵語

 ENG × 普通話

range hood (n.)
抽油煙機

laundry
detergent (n.)
洗衣液

oven glove (n.)
隔熱手套

bottle opener (n.)
開瓶器

toaster (n.)
多士爐
（烤麵包機）

stir-fry (v.)
炒

saucepan (n.)
深平底鍋

kettle (n.)
電熱水煲
（電熱水壺）

stove (n.)
爐灶

wok (n.)
鑊

microwave (n.)
微波爐

frying pan (n.)
平底煎鍋

apron (n.)
圍裙

oven (n.)
焗爐（烤箱

washing machine (n.)
洗衣機

mix (v.)
混合

pour (v.)
倒進

kitchen roll (n.)
廚房紙

whisk (n.) 攪拌器
(v.) 攪拌

peel (v.)
削皮

season (v.)
調味

Let's Talk

Q: How can you help in the kitchen ?
A: I can whisk eggs.

Q: What should you be careful of when
you are in the kitchen ?
A: I should be careful of sharp objects.

Daily English

當我們要洗碗碟時，一般會説 do the
dishes，而不説 wash。例如：It's
my turn to do the dishes tonight.
（今晚輪到我洗碗碟。）

14

dishcloth (n.)
洗碗布

scouring pad (n.)
百潔布

washing-up liquid (n.)
洗潔精

cupboard (n.)
櫥櫃

put away
放好

sink (n.) 洗碗槽

dish rack (n.) 乾碟架

refrigerator-freezer (n.) 雙門雪櫃（雙門冰箱）

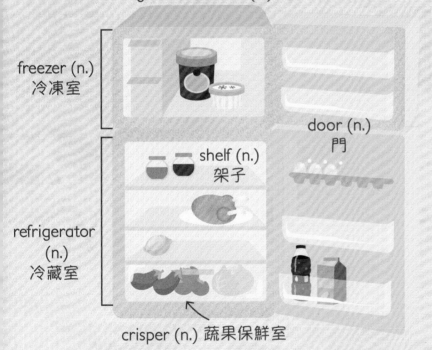

freezer (n.)
冷凍室

door (n.)
門

shelf (n.)
架子

refrigerator (n.)
冷藏室

crisper (n.) 蔬果保鮮室

cut (v.) 切

kitchen knife (n.)
菜刀

chopping board (n.)
砧板

grate (v.)
磨碎

grater (n.)
磨碎器

⚠ Rules to Know

媽媽正在做什麼？原來她在廚房裏做飯，那就可以把動作變成現在進行式來說明，例如：
- Mom is cooking now.
- Mom is preparing the food now.

😆 Fun Corner

Wok 這字詞來自廣東話「鑊」的發音。這種中國的煮食工具傳到外國後，外國人直接以「鑊」的發音作為它的英文名稱。

Face and emotion
表情和情緒

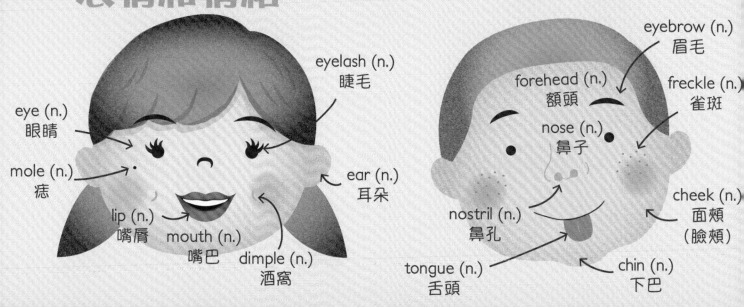

eyelash (n.) 睫毛

eye (n.) 眼睛

mole (n.) 痣

ear (n.) 耳朵

lip (n.) 嘴脣

mouth (n.) 嘴巴

dimple (n.) 酒窩

eyebrow (n.) 眉毛

forehead (n.) 額頭

freckle (n.) 雀斑

nose (n.) 鼻子

nostril (n.) 鼻孔

cheek (n.) 面頰（臉頰）

tongue (n.) 舌頭

chin (n.) 下巴

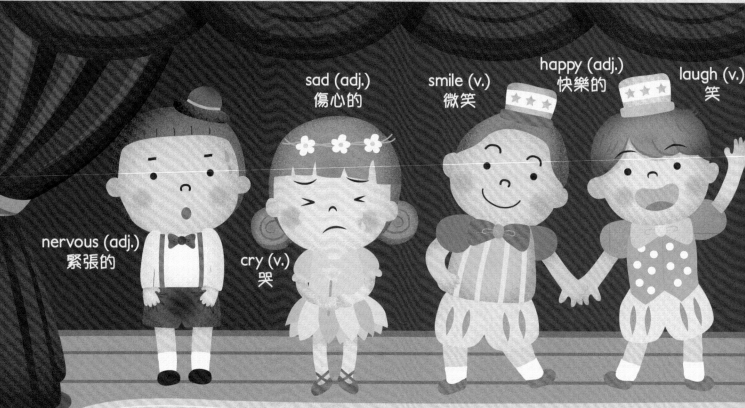

sad (adj.) 傷心的

smile (v.) 微笑

happy (adj.) 快樂的

laugh (v.) 笑

nervous (adj.) 緊張的

cry (v.) 哭

💬 Let's Talk

Q: How do you feel when you...
- perform on stage ?
- meet a new friend ?

A: I feel...
- nervous when I perform on stage.
- shy when I meet a new friend.

💬 Daily English

朋友不開心時，我們可以說什麼來鼓勵他們呢？
- Cheer up !
- Be happy !
- Keep your chin up !
- Don't lose heart !

to raise one's eyebrows
揚起眉毛

surprised (adj.)
驚訝的

to roll one's eyes
翻白眼

annoyed (adj.)
感到厭煩的

to purse one's lips
撅嘴

angry (adj.)
生氣的

shy (adj.)
害羞的

scared (adj.)
害怕的

excited (adj.)
興奮的

bored (adj.)
無聊的

⚠ Rules to Know

我們會用形容詞來表達內心的各種
感受，例如：
- I am angry.（生氣）
- Judy was happy when she
  won the game.（快樂）

😆 Fun Corner

英文裏有時會用顏色來代替不同的心情或表情，
例如：
- I feel blue.（當感到悲傷時）
- His face turns red.（當感到憤怒或尷尬時）
- She is in the pink.（看來容光煥發）

17

Action words
一起做動作！

😀 Let's Talk

Q: Are you ticklish?
A: Yes, I am. I laugh if someone tickles me.

Q: What is the funniest face you can make? Talk about it and act it out.

💬 Daily English

有些動作能夠反映我們的狀態，例如疲累可以用以下句子來表達：
- I couldn't stop yawning.
  我不斷打哈欠。
- I can hardly keep my eyes open.
  我的眼睛快張不開了。

⚠ Rules to Know

我們可以用副詞來具體地描述動作是怎樣的，例如：
- Hailey yawned deeply.
  （深深地打哈欠）
- Mark stamped his foot angrily.（生氣地用力踏腳）

😆 Fun Corner

打電話或接電話這兩個動作都是 pick up the phone，但表示別人在通電話卻會説成 on the phone。

giggle (v.) 咯咯地笑

tickle (v.) 給別人搔癢

ticklish (adj.) 怕癢的

high five 舉手擊掌

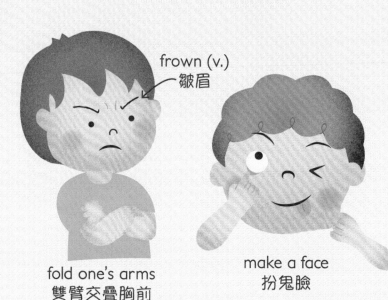

frown (v.) 皺眉

fold one's arms 雙臂交疊胸前

make a face 扮鬼臉

twist (v.)
扭動

I dance with my arms akimbo.
我叉着腰跳舞。

stamp (v.)
用力踏腳

wink (v.)
眨眼

hand in hand
手牽手

tiptoe (v.)
踮腳尖

squat down
蹲下

shrug (v.)
聳肩

hold one's nose
捏住鼻子

daydream (n.)
白日夢

snore (v.)
打鼾

yawn (v.) 打哈欠

nod off 打瞌睡

hiccup (v.)
打嗝

Body 身體

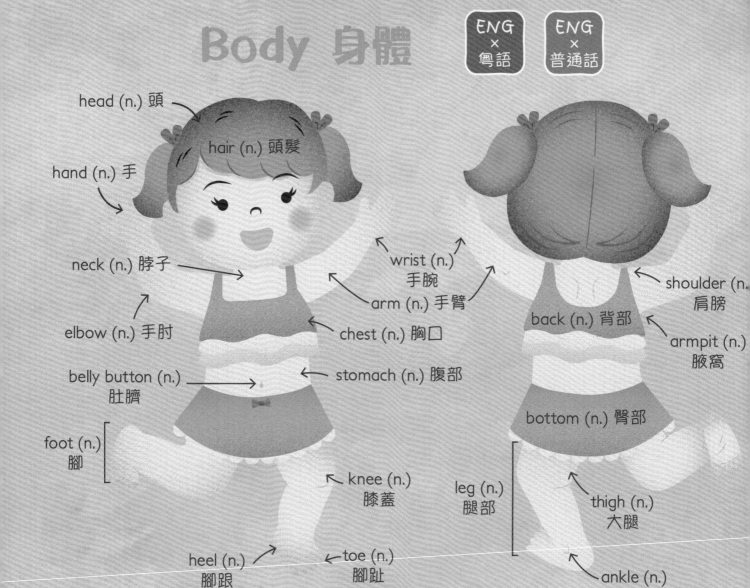

head (n.) 頭
hair (n.) 頭髮
hand (n.) 手
neck (n.) 脖子
elbow (n.) 手肘
belly button (n.) 肚臍
foot (n.) 腳
wrist (n.) 手腕
arm (n.) 手臂
chest (n.) 胸口
stomach (n.) 腹部
knee (n.) 膝蓋
heel (n.) 腳跟
toe (n.) 腳趾
leg (n.) 腿部
shoulder (n.) 肩膀
armpit (n.) 腋窩
back (n.) 背部
bottom (n.) 臀部
thigh (n.) 大腿
ankle (n.) 腳踝

bob (n.) 齊耳短髮
skinhead (n.) 平頭
curly (adj.) 鬈曲的 [頭髮]
bangs (n.) 劉海
straight (adj.) 直直的 [頭髮]
fat (adj.) 胖胖的

middle finger (n.) 中指

ring finger (n.) 無名指

little finger (n.) 小指

fingerprint (n.) 指紋

index finger (n.) 食指

finger (n.) 手指

thumb (n.) 拇指

fingernail (n.) 指甲

palm (n.) 手掌

see (v.) 看

taste (v.) 品嘗

smell (v.) 嗅

hear (v.) 聽

touch (v.) 觸摸

bun (n.) 圓髮髻

bald (adj.) 禿頭的

What's your name?

tall (adj.) 高高的

moustache (n.) 鬍子

I'm Kelly.

ponytail (n.) 馬尾

thin (adj.) 瘦瘦的

short (adj.) 矮小的

Let's Talk

Q: What does Kelly look like?

A: She wears her hair in a ponytail.

Q: How tall are you? How much do you weigh?

A: I am 90 cm tall. I weigh 18 kg.

Daily English

我們常常用 fat 去形容別人身形肥胖，但其實這個字詞含有貶義，不太禮貌，可以改為説：

• Look at this chubby boy!
• Mr. Chan is a big man.

Rules to Know

有些身體部分的單數和複數拼法很不一樣，例如：

• foot（單數） ⟶ feet（複數）
• tooth（單數） ⟶ teeth（複數）

Fun Corner

我們平時會豎起拇指來讚賞別人，在英文裏也會用 'Thumbs up.' 生動地表示這個動作。相反，'Thumbs down.' 就是不讚許的意思。

Clothes and accessories
衣服和飾物

backpack (n.)
背包

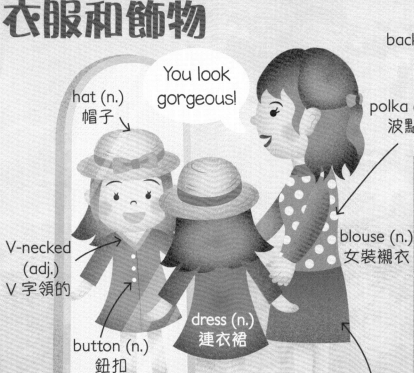

hat (n.)
帽子

You look gorgeous!

polka dots (n.)
波點圖案

blouse (n.)
女裝襯衣

V-necked (adj.)
V 字領的

button (n.)
鈕扣

dress (n.)
連衣裙

skirt (n.)
裙子

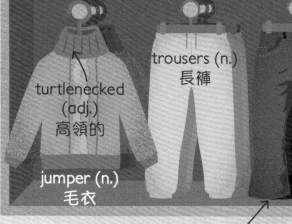

turtlenecked (adj.)
高領的

trousers (n.)
長褲

jumper (n.)
毛衣

jeans (n.) 牛仔褲

sandals (n.) high heels (n.)　boots (n.) 靴子
涼鞋　　　　高跟鞋

trainers (n.) leather shoes (n.)　flip-flops (n.)
運動鞋　　　　皮鞋　　　　人字拖鞋

shoelaces (n.) 鞋帶

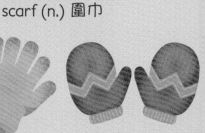

scarf (n.) 圍巾

gloves (n.) 手套　　mittens (n.) 手套

🐣 Let's Talk

Q: What is the little girl wearing ?
A: The little girl is wearing a dress.

Q: What do you wear when it is warm ?
A: I wear a T-shirt when it is warm.

💬 Daily English

當別人打扮得很漂亮時，可以這樣稱讚他們：
- You look fantastic !
- You look gorgeous !
- I really like your outfit.

fitting room (n.) 試衣室（試衣間）

take off 脫下

andbag (n.) 袋（手包）

tie (n.) 領帶

cap (n.) 鴨舌帽

belt (n.) 腰帶

shirt (n.) 襯衣

vest (n.) 背心

stripes (n.) 條紋

T-shirt (n.) T 恤

shorts (n.) 短褲

crewneck (adj.) 圓領的

put on 穿上

jacket (n.) 短上衣

underpants (n.) 內褲

socks (n.) 襪子

hairband (n.) 頭箍

hair tie (n.) 髮圈

hair slide (n.) 小髮夾

ring (n.) 戒指

earring (n.) 耳環

bracelet (n.) 手鐲

necklace (n.) 項鏈

! Rules to Know

一雙襪子是 a pair of socks，一雙鞋子是 a pair of shoes。但有些衣物明明不是「一雙」，卻要用複數來表示，例如：
• 一條短褲是 a pair of shorts；
• 一條長褲是 a pair of trousers。

☺ Fun Corner

長褲的英式英文是 trousers，在美國則叫作 pants。可是，pants 這個字詞在英式英文中卻指內褲。

23

Fruit and vegetables
水果和蔬菜

carrot (n.) 胡蘿蔔

pak choi (n.) 白菜

give change
找續（找錢）

weigh (v.)
秤重

basket (n.)
籃子

potato (n.)
馬鈴薯

eggplant (n.) 茄子

apple (n.)
蘋果

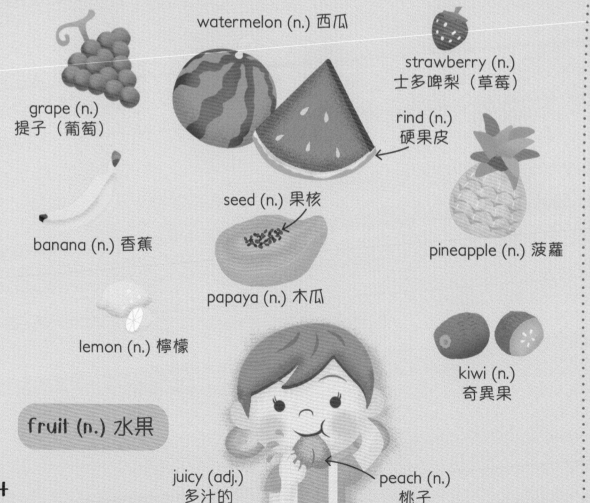

watermelon (n.) 西瓜

strawberry (n.)
士多啤梨（草莓）

grape (n.)
提子（葡萄）

rind (n.)
硬果皮

cauliflower (
椰菜花（花菜

seed (n.) 果核

banana (n.) 香蕉

pineapple (n.) 菠蘿

papaya (n.) 木瓜

lemon (n.) 檸檬

kiwi (n.)
奇異果

broccoli (n.)
西蘭花

fruit (n.) 水果

juicy (adj.)
多汁的

peach (n.)
桃子

green (adj.)
未熟的

market (n.) 市場

pay (v.) 付錢

orange (n.) 橙

pear (n.) 梨子

crunchy (adj.) 爽脆的

CHOMP!

fresh (adj.) 新鮮的

pea (n.) 豌豆

onion (n.) 洋蔥

spring onion (n.) 蔥

choy sum / flowering Chinese cabbage (n.) 菜心

corn (n.) 粟米（玉米）

cucumber (n.) 青瓜（黃瓜）

tomato (n.) 番茄

ripe (adj.) 成熟的

vegetables (n.) 蔬菜

🗨 Let's Talk

Q: What fruit do you like to snack on ?

A: Strawberries and oranges.

Q: Why are fruit and vegetables important to us ?

A: Because they are good for our health.

💬 Daily English

除了 yummy 外，我們還可以怎樣表達食物真美味呢？
• Yum!
• It tastes so good!
• It's tasty / delicious!

⚠ Rules to Know

圖中有多少蘋果？答案是 6 個，即 six apples。如果蘋果的數量超過一個，我們就要在 apple 後面加上 s。一起看看其他例子：
• a pear → five pears
• a carrot → four carrots
• a potato → five potatoes
• a cherry → two cherries

😆 Fun Corner

Amy is the apple of her dad's eye. 一句中的 Amy 並不是蘋果，而是她爸爸的心肝寶貝。

Food and drinks I love
喜愛的食物和飲品

ENG × 粵語
ENG × 普通話

bakery (n.) 麵包店

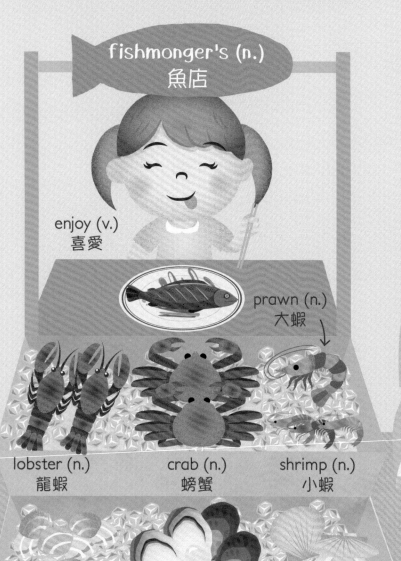

fishmonger's (n.) 魚店

enjoy (v.) 喜愛

prawn (n.) 大蝦

lobster (n.) 龍蝦

crab (n.) 螃蟹

shrimp (n.) 小蝦

clam (n.) 蜆

oyster (n.) 蠔

scallop (n.) 扇貝

cream (n.) 忌廉（奶油）

muffin (n.) 鬆餅

cake (n.) 蛋糕

fruit tart (n.) 水果餡餅

apple pie (n.) 蘋果 （蘋果派）

biscuit (n.) 餅乾

bread (n.) 麵包

🫦 Let's Talk

Q: What is your favourite snack?
A: My favourite snack is chocolate.

Q: What will happen if you eat too much meat or seafood?
A: I will have a stomach ache.

💬 Daily English

肚子餓了，我們可以怎麼說呢？
• I am hungry.
• My stomach is growling.
如果已經餓得不得了，就要說：
• I am starving.
• I am ravenous.

snack shop (n.) 零食店

straw (n.)
飲管
（吸管）

slurp (v.)
咕嘟地喝

fizzy (adj.)
有氣的

soft drink (n.) 汽水　juice (n.) 果汁

chocolate (n.)
朱古力（巧克力）

marshmallow (n.)
棉花糖

ice cream (n.)
雪糕（冰淇淋）

ice lolly (n.)
雪條（冰棒）

lollipop (n.)
棒棒糖

**butcher's (n.)
肉店**

raw (adj.)
生的

cooked (adj.)
煮熟的

beef (n.)
牛肉

steak (n.)
牛排

pork (n.)
豬肉

pork chop (n.)
豬排

sausage (n.)
香腸

chicken (n.)
雞肉

drumstick (n.)
雞槌（雞腿）

chicken wing (n.)
雞翅膀

⚠ Rules to Know

我們不會説 one chocolate，如要提及它的數量，可用以下方法：

• **One bar of chocolate**
一條朱古力（巧克力）

• **One box of chocolate**
一盒朱古力（巧克力）

😆 Fun Corner

不少零食也有英式和美式的名稱。在不同地方，要使用不同的叫法呢！

• 餅乾：英 biscuit / 美 cookie
• 糖果：英 sweet / 美 candy
• 薯片：英 crisps / 美 potato chips
• 炸薯條：英 chips / 美 fries

Plants 植物

sunlight (n.) 陽光

tree (n.) 樹

fruit (n.) 果實
(v.) 結果

fragrant (adj.) 芳香的

bark (n.) 樹皮

fall (v.) 落下

nest (n.) 巢

leaf (n.) 樹葉

branch (n.) 樹枝

trunk (n.) 樹幹

thorn (n.) 刺

rose (n.) 玫瑰

fern (n.) 蕨類植物

grass (n.) 草

stem (n.) 莖

mushroom (n.) 蘑菇

moss (n.) 苔蘚

soil (n.) 泥土

root (n.) 根

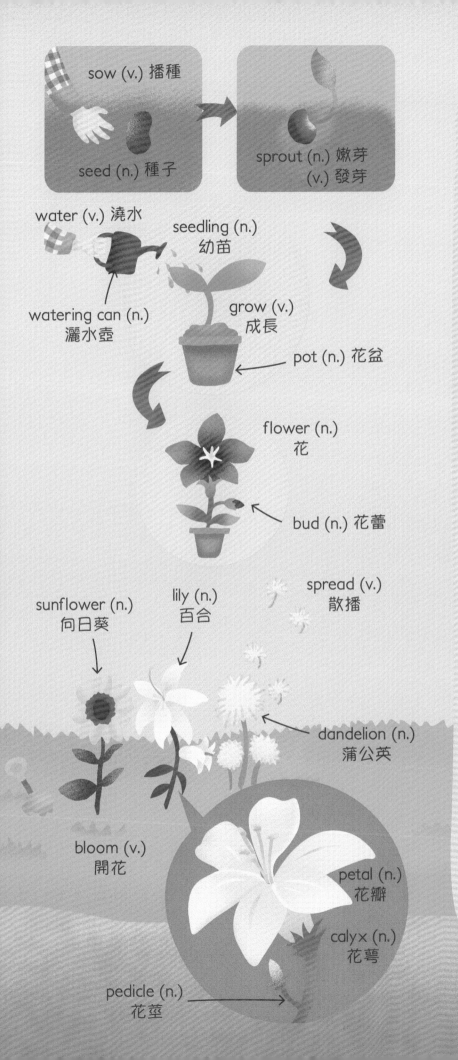

sow (v.) 播種

seed (n.) 種子

sprout (n.) 嫩芽
(v.) 發芽

water (v.) 澆水

seedling (n.)
幼苗

watering can (n.)
灑水壺

grow (v.)
成長

pot (n.) 花盆

flower (n.)
花

bud (n.) 花蕾

spread (v.)
散播

sunflower (n.)
向日葵

lily (n.)
百合

dandelion (n.)
蒲公英

bloom (v.)
開花

petal (n.)
花瓣

calyx (n.)
花萼

pedicle (n.)
花莖

Let's Talk

Q: What flower colours do you like?

A: I like yellow flowers.

Q: What should we do to take care of a plant?

A: We should water it, and put it in the sun.

Daily English

我們可以怎樣描述各種各樣的樹呢？

• a tall tree 高高的樹
• a leafy tree 茂盛的樹
• a bald tree 光禿禿的樹

Rules to Know

當我們用幾個形容詞來描述一朵花時，中英文的排列次序可能不同！例如：「一朵漂亮的粉紅色小花」是 a beautiful, little, pink flower。在英文中，要先說出意見，然後描述大小，再提及顏色。

Fun Corner

Root and branch 字面的意思是根和樹枝，但合起來卻指徹底地，例如：She has cleaned her room root and branch. 表示她把房間徹底地打掃乾淨。

29

Farm animals and pets
農場動物和寵物

farmhouse (n.) 農舍

barn (n.) 糧倉

orchard (n.) 果園

Oink! 噏！

pig (n.) 豬

farmer (n.) 牧場主人

trough (n.) 飼料槽

pen (n.) 豬欄

dog (n.) 狗

cat (n.) 貓

rat (n.) 大老鼠

Quack! 嘎！

duck (n.) 鴨

goose (n.) 鵝

goat (n.) 山羊

Baa! 咩！

feed an animal 餵飼動物

Let's Talk

Q: Have you ever fed an animal?
A: Yes, I have. I have fed a goat. / No, I haven't.

Q: Do you have a pet?
A: Yes, I do. I have a puppy. / No, I don't.

Daily English

從圖中找出各種農場動物的叫聲，模仿牠們叫一叫吧！

Moo!

coop (n.) 雞舍

rooster (n.) 公雞

hen (n.) 母雞

chicken (n.) 雞

Moo! 哞！

cow (n.) 牛

Cluck! 喔！

← egg (n.) 蛋

milk a cow 擠牛奶

horse (n.) 馬

Neigh! 嘶！

stable (n.) 馬廄

donkey (n.) 驢

hay (n.) 乾草

shear a sheep 剪羊毛

wool (n.) 羊毛

sheep (n.) 綿羊

⚠ Rules to Know

我們稱呼動物的寶寶時，除了在動物名稱前加上 baby 外（如 baby chicken），還會有其他叫法呢！例如：
- chick 小雞
- duckling 小鴨
- gosling 小鵝
- calf 小牛
- piglet 小豬
- foal 小馬
- kitten 小貓
- puppy 小狗
- lamb 小綿羊
- kid 小山羊

😆 Fun Corner

Hold your horses. 可以是請牧場主人拉住馬匹，但也有請別人停下來想清楚的意思。

Wild animals 野生動物

Bleat!
嗚！

giraffe (n.)
長頸鹿

monkey (n.)
猴子

beak (n.)
喙

tail (n.) 尾巴

woodpecker (n.)
啄木鳥

tiger (n.) 老虎

dangle (v.)
來回擺動

sleepy (adj.)
昏昏欲睡的

koala (n.)
樹熊
（樹袋熊）

spine (n.)
刺

Roar!
吼！

hedgehog (n.)
刺蝟

rabbit (n.)
兔子

furry (adj.)
有毛皮的

stump (n.)
樹頭（樹樁）

bear (n.) 熊

snake (n.)
蛇

frog (n.) 青蛙

hump (n.)
駝峯

savannah (n.)
稀樹草原

desert (n.)
沙漠

stripes (n.)
斑紋

tadpole
(n.)
蝌蚪

camel (n.)
駱駝

zebra (n.)
斑馬

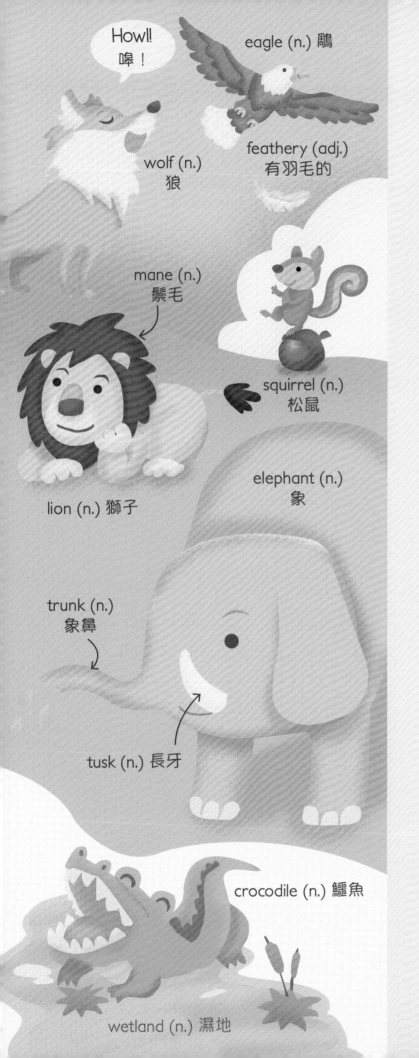

Howl!
嗥！

eagle (n.) 鷳

feathery (adj.)
有羽毛的

wolf (n.)
狼

mane (n.)
鬃毛

squirrel (n.)
松鼠

lion (n.) 獅子

elephant (n.)
象

trunk (n.)
象鼻

tusk (n.) 長牙

crocodile (n.) 鱷魚

wetland (n.) 濕地

😮 Let's Talk

Q: What colour is the wolf?
A: The wolf is grey.

Q: What animals have wings / fur / etc.?
A: Eagles have wings. / Bears have fur.

💬 Daily English

森林裏的動物究竟會發出什麼聲音？大家來模仿牠們叫一叫吧！
• 長頸鹿的叫聲：Bleat!
• 狼的嚎叫：Howl!
• 熊的咆哮：Roar!

❗ Rules to Know

每種動物都有不同的能力，真厲害！我們可以用 can 來說明牠們會做的事情，例如：
• Eagles can fly.
  鷹會飛。
• Snakes can slide.
  蛇會滑行。

😆 Fun Corner

動物名稱有不同的性別，例如 lion and lioness 分別是雄獅和母獅，而 tiger and tigress 就是雄老虎和雌老虎。

Sea animals 海洋生物

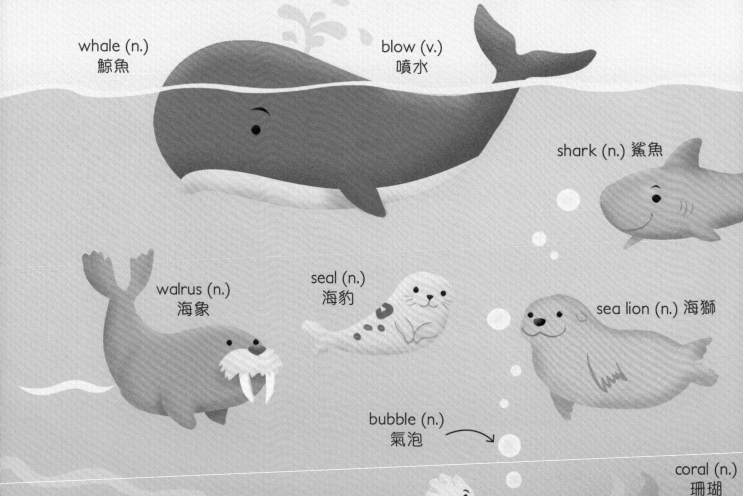

whale (n.) 鯨魚

blow (v.) 噴水

shark (n.) 鯊魚

walrus (n.) 海象

seal (n.) 海豹

sea lion (n.) 海獅

bubble (n.) 氣泡

coral (n.) 珊瑚

jellyfish (n.) 水母

seahorse (n.) 海馬

cuttlefish (n.) 墨魚

quiet (adj.) 安靜的

starfish (n.) 海星

octopus (n.) 八爪魚

seabed (n.) 海牀

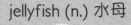

seaweed (n.) 海草

seagull (n.)
海鷗

calm (adj.) 風平浪靜的

fin (n.) 鰭

dolphin (n.)
海豚

turtle (n.)
海龜

diver (n.)
潛水員

dive (v.) 潛水

wetsuit (n.)
潛水衣

swimfins (n.)
蛙鞋

clownfish (n.)
小丑魚

submarine (n.)
潛水艇

🗣 Let's Talk

Q: Have you ever swum in the sea?

A: Yes, I have. / No, I haven't.

Q: Can you name three sea animals in the picture that have fins?

A: The dolphin, the whale and the clownfish have fins.

💬 Daily English

你會怎樣描述這片海洋呢？請用以下句式說一說。

The ocean is...
• huge (adj.) 巨大的
• glassy (adj.) 明亮的
• beautiful (adj.) 美麗的

⚠ Rules to Know

海洋裏有不少生物都是複合詞，那是由兩個字詞組成的，例如：
• 海草 seaweed = sea + weed
• 海星 starfish = star + fish
• 海馬 seahorse = sea + horse

😆 Fun Corner

Turtle 看起來和 tortoise 差不多，人們常常弄錯牠們。其實在水裏或近岸地方生活的龜叫 turtle（海龜），而在陸上生活的則叫 tortoise（陸龜）。

35

Insects 昆蟲

dragonfly (n.) 蜻蜓

moth (n.) 飛蛾

sweep net (n.)
捕蟲網

antenna (n.)
觸角

snail (n.)
蝸牛

cricket (n.) 蟋蟀

pond (n.) 池塘

grasshopper (n.)
草蜢（蚱蜢）

ladybug / ladybird (n.)
瓢蟲

centipede (n.)
蜈蚣

beetle (n.)
甲蟲

worm (n.) 蟲

life cycle (n.) 生命周期

egg (n.)
卵

caterpillar (n.)
毛蟲

cocoon (n.)
繭

butterfly (n.)
蝴蝶

anthill (n.) 蟻丘

ant (n.) 螞蟻

bee (n.) 蜜蜂

beehive (n.) 蜂巢

spider (n.) 蜘蛛

spider web (n.) 蜘蛛網

firefly (n.) 螢火蟲

fly (n.) 蒼蠅

bite (v.) 咬

mosquito (n.) 蚊子

cockroach (n.) 蟑螂

Let's Talk

Q: Which insects are flying?
A: The moth and the dragonfly are flying.

Q: Do you like insects?
A: Yes, I like insects. / No, I am afraid of insects.

Daily English

以下形容詞會讓人想起什麼昆蟲呢？請説一説。
• tiny 細小的
• slimy 黏乎乎的
• wiggly 扭動的

Rules to Know

昆蟲住在哪兒？我們可以用 in 來表示牠們居住的地方。
• Ants live in anthills.
  螞蟻住在蟻丘。
• Bees live in beehives.
  蜜蜂住在蜂巢。

Fun Corner

我們可以用不同的昆蟲來作生動的比喻，例如：
• as busy as a bee
  （像蜜蜂一樣）忙碌
• as merry as a cricket
  （像蟋蟀一樣）快樂

Festivals
節日

Chinese New Year 農曆新年

lion dance (n.) 舞獅

red banner (n.) 揮春

出入平安

Happy New Year!

Chinese candy box (n.) 攢盒

glutinous rice cake (n.) 年糕

red packet (n.) 紅包

Mid-Autumn Festival 中秋節

full moon (n.) 滿月

lantern riddle (n.) 燈謎

moon cake (n.) 月餅

guess (v.) 猜

lantern (n.) 燈籠

enjoy the full moon 賞月

Have a great holiday!

rice dumpling (n.) 粽子

Easter 復活節

Happy Easter!

basket (n.) 籃子

Easter bunny (n.) 復活兔

Easter egg (n.) 復活蛋

dragon boat (n.) 龍舟

flag (n.) 旗子

drummer (n.) 鼓手　paddler (n.) 划槳手

Dragon Boat Festival 端午節

38

Halloween 萬聖節

spider web (n.) 蜘蛛網

Trick or treat?

jack-o'-lantern (n.) 南瓜燈

pumpkin (n.) 南瓜

candy (n.) 糖果

costume (n.) 戲服

Christmas tree (n.) 聖誕樹

Christmas stocking (n.) 聖誕襪

gingerbread man (n.) 薑餅人

Merry Christmas!

turkey (n.) 火雞

string lights (n.) 燈串

present (n.) 禮物

Santa Claus (n.) 聖誕老人

Christmas 聖誕節

Let's Talk

Q: Which of these are western festivals? And which are Chinese festivals?
(Let's check it out!)

Q: What is your favourite festival? Why?

A: My favourite festival is Christmas because I can meet Santa Claus.

Daily English

在這些節日時，我們應說什麼應節的話？在圖中看一看。

Rules to Know

提及聖誕節的節目時，小心引起誤會！

• 聖誕期間：We are travelling to Europe at Christmas.

• 聖誕節當天：We will have a party on Christmas Day.

Fun Corner

有些中式節日有其他英文名稱，例如：

• 中秋節跟月亮息息相關，因此這天又稱為 Moon Festival。

• 中國新年是以農曆 Lunar Calendar 計算，因此又叫 Lunar New Year。

Special days 特別的日子

pennant banner (n.) 三角旗橫額

confetti popper (n.) 彩帶拉炮

party hat (n.) 派對帽

birthday card (n.) 生日卡

HAPPY BIRTHDAY

balloon (n.) 氣球

HAPPY BIRTHDAY

birthday cake (n.) 生日蛋糕

birthday party (n.) 生日派對

throw the confetti 拋五彩碎紙

mortarboard (n.) 畢業帽

certificate (n.) 證書

gown (n.) 袍

Graduation Ceremony 畢業禮

kiss (v.) 親吻

carnation (n.) 康乃馨

bouquet (n.) 花束

Mother's Day 母親節

40

ribbon (n.) 緞帶

party bag (n.) 禮物袋

light the candles 點蠟燭

wrap (v.) 包

blow out the candles 吹蠟燭

present (n.) 禮物

clap (v.) 拍手

make a wish 許願

take a photo 拍照

hug (v.) 擁抱

HAPPY FATHER DAY

bow tie (n.) 蝶形領結

Father's Day 父親節

Let's Talk

Q: How old is the little girl in the picture? How do you know that?

A: She is five years old. There are five candles on the cake.

Q: What do you do at a birthday party?

A: We sing at a birthday party.

Daily English

參加生日派對真開心！除了用 happy 來表達這種心情外，還可以使用以下的形容詞：
- delighted
- cheerful
- glad
- joyful
- contented
- pleased

Rules to Know

父親節和母親節這些特別的日子都是專有名詞，所以每個字詞的第一個英文字母要使用大寫呢！
- Mother's Day
- Father's Day

Fun Corner

Throw a party 是指舉行派對，大家不要以為是「拋」出派對啊！

Classroom 課室

bulletin board (n.) 壁報板

blackboard (n.) 黑板

ask a question 提問問題

How do you spell 'classroom'?

raise one's hand 舉手

textbo... (n.) 課本

teacher (n.) 老師

letters (n.) 字母

student (n.) 學生

chat (v...) 聊天

duster (n.) 黑板擦

chalk (n.) 粉筆

read (v.) 閱讀

bin (n.) 垃圾桶

desk (n.) 書桌

computer (n.) 電腦

number (n.) 數字

stationery (n.) 文具

1314

screen (n.) 屏幕

pencil (n.) 鉛筆

ruler (n.) 尺子

keyboard (n.) 鍵盤

mouse (n.) 滑鼠

pen (n.) 筆

42

painting (n.)
圖畫

whiteboard (n.)
白板

take out one's book
拿出課本

Keep quiet, please!

schoolbag (n.)
書包

uniform (n.)
校服

write (v.) 寫

pencil case (n.)
筆盒

eraser (n.)
橡皮

glue (n.)
膠水

highlighter (n.)
螢光筆

scissors (n.) 剪刀

Recess 小息

basketball court (n.) 籃球場

covered playground (n.)
有蓋操場

talk (v.) 談話

locker (n.)
儲物櫃

read the book
看書

eat a snack
吃零食

skip rope 跳繩

tuck shop (n.) 小食部

line up 排隊

cooked food (n.)
熟食

buy a snack
買零食

snack (n.) 零食

queue (n.) 隊伍

44

Let's play games!

ball (n.) 皮球

play catch 拋擲遊戲

fun (adj.) 令人愉快的

the ground (n.) 地面

canned drink (n.) 罐裝飲品

$5　SOLD OUT　$8

coin (n.) 硬幣

INSERT COIN

insert (v.) 放入

vending machine (n.) 自動販賣機

Let's Talk

Q: How many children are lining up at the tuck shop?

A: Four children are lining up at the tuck shop.

Q: What do you usually do at recess?

A: I usually play with my friends.

Daily English

我們應怎樣邀請同學一起玩耍呢?
- Shall we play?
- Let's play games!
- Do you want to play with us?

Rules to Know

小息時,我們通常會到小食部買食物來吃。這時就可以用 some (一些) 來表示食物的分量,例如:
- I bought some snacks.
- I ate some cookies at recess.

Fun Corner

除了 recess 外,我們還可以用 break 來表示短暫的休息時間。例如我們會説 Let's take a break. 來提議大家小休一下。

45

Supermarket 超級市場

ENG × 粵語　ENG × 普通話

toiletries (n.) 洗漱用品

household product (n.) 家居用品

dairy product (n.) 奶類製品

shopping basket (n.) 購物籃

frozen food (n.) 冷藏食品

meat (n.) 肉類

aisle (n.) 通道

cart (n.) 手推車

produce (n.) 農產品

rice (n.) 米

noodles (n.) 麵條

checkstand (n.) 收銀櫃枱

cashier (n.) 收銀員

cash register (n.) 收銀機

sauce (n.) 醬料

confectionery (n.) 甜點

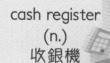

give chan 找續（找錢

beverage (n.) 飲品

snack and nuts (n.) 零食和果仁

customer (n.) 顧客

bakery product (n.) 烘焙食品

seafood (n.) 海鮮

tin and can (n.) 罐頭食品

self-checkout counter (n.) 自動收銀櫃枱

pack (v.) 包裝

grocery bag (n.) 購物袋

👄 Let's Talk

Q: Where can you find the bread?

A: I can find the bread in the bakery section.

Q: What do you usually buy at the supermarket?

A: I usually buy cheese and milk.

💬 Daily English

到超級市場購買食物和日用品一般叫 do grocery shopping，又可以説 buy groceries。

⚠ Rules to Know

我們通常會在超級市場裏買很多東西，這時可用 a lot of 來表示「很多」，例如：

- I want to buy a lot of bananas.
  我想買很多香蕉。
- We need a lot of meat.
  我們需要很多肉。

😆 Fun Corner

在超級市場裏的手推車除了叫 cart 外，還可以叫 trolley。

Restaurant
餐廳

ENG × 粵語
ENG × 普通話

carry the tray
拿托盤

serve the meal
上菜

wallet (n.)
錢包

pay the bill 結賬

waitress (n.) 女侍應

order (v.)
點菜

take the order
記下點的菜

napkin (n.)
餐巾

condiment (n.)
調味料

menu (n.)
菜單

waiter (n.)
侍應

clear the dishe
清理碗碟

🗣 Let's Talk

Q: Do you like to eat out? Why?
A: Yes, I do. Because I can try different dishes.

Q: What should you not do when you are in a restaurant?
A: I should not talk with my mouth full.

💬 Daily English

在餐廳裏，我們應該怎樣點菜呢？
• I'd like a hamburger, please.
  我想要漢堡包，謝謝。
• Do you have any cakes?
  這裏有蛋糕嗎？

48

Menu

Appetizer 前菜

salad (n.) 沙律（沙拉）

Side Dish 配菜

mashed potato (n.)
馬鈴薯蓉

Main Course 主菜

pasta (n.) 意大利麵

hamburger (n.) 漢堡包

deep-fried chicken leg (n.)
炸雞腿

Dessert 甜品

Cheese cake (n.)
芝士蛋糕

Drinks 飲品

tea (n.) 茶

---

fast food restaurant (n.)
快餐店

soft drink (n.)
汽水

Chinese restaurant (n.)
中菜餐廳／酒樓

dim sum (n.)
點心

café (n.)
咖啡室

coffee (n.)
咖啡

⚠ Rules to Know

動詞和介詞組合起來，可以變出很多有趣的意思！
大家看看這些常見的例子：

- eat out　在外吃飯
- eat in　　在家吃飯
- eat up　　吃光

😝 Fun Corner

Pasta 是意大利麵的統稱，大家最熟悉的意大利長麵 spaghetti 只是其中一種，常見的還有蝴蝶粉 farfalle、通心粉 macaroni 和千層麵 lasagna。

Help! 救命！

ENG × 粵語　ENG × 普通話

1

rob (v.) 搶劫
robber (n.) 盜賊

2

police officer (n.) 警察
walkie-talkie (n.) 對講機

police car (n.) 警車
siren (n.) 警報器
POLICE

3

gun (n.) 槍
truncheon (n.) 警棍
chase (v.) 追捕
escape (v.) 逃走

4

arrest (v.) 拘捕
handcuffs (n.) 手銬

5

POLICE STATION 警察局
police dog (n.) 警犬

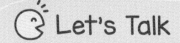

🗣 Let's Talk

Q: Have you ever visited a police station or a fire station?

A: Yes, I have visited a fire station. / No, I haven't.

Q: What makes a good firefighter?

A: A good firefighter has to be strong and brave.

💬 Daily English

發生緊急的事情時，除了大叫救命外，還可以怎樣求助呢？

• I need help!
我需要幫助！

• We've got an emergency!
這裏發生了緊急事故！

/go off 響

smoke (n.) 煙

fire (n.) 火

burn (v.) 燃燒

fire alarm (n.) 火警鐘

2

3

Help! 救命！

cry out 叫喊

DANGEROUS (adj.) 危險

dial (v.) 撥號

999

firefighter (n.) 消防員

aerial ladder (n.) 雲梯

put out the fire 滅火

fire engine (n.) 消防車

5

rescue (v.) 救援

helmet (n.) 頭盔

hydrant (n.) 消防栓

hose (n.) 滅火喉

axe (n.) 斧頭

fire extinguisher (n.) 滅火器

⚠ Rules to Know

提及發生火警的注意事項時，可以在句中
加上 must，例如：

- You **must** stay calm.
  你必須保持冷靜。
- You **must** not use a lift.
  你一定不能使用升降機。

😝 Fun Corner

消防員可以稱為 firefighter，男性消防
員可以稱為 fireman，而女性則可以稱
為 firewoman。警察可以稱為 police
officer，男性警察可以稱為 policeman，
而女性則可以稱為 policewoman。

Clinic 診所

ENG × 粵語　ENG × 普通話

symptoms 症狀

Let's go to the doctor.
一起去看醫生吧。

headache (n.) 頭痛

stuffy nose (n.) 鼻塞

sore throat (n.) 喉嚨痛

cold (n.) 感冒

stomach ache (n.) 腹痛

vomit (v.) 嘔吐

dizzy (adj.) 頭暈

diarrhea (n.) 腹瀉

shaky (adj.) 發抖的

CLINIC

wait (v.) 等候

examine one's throat
檢查喉嚨

receptionist (n.)
接待員

thermometer (n.)
溫度計

sick / ill (adj.)
生病的

register (v.)
登記

take one's
temperature
探熱
（量體溫）

examination
table (n.)
診斷牀

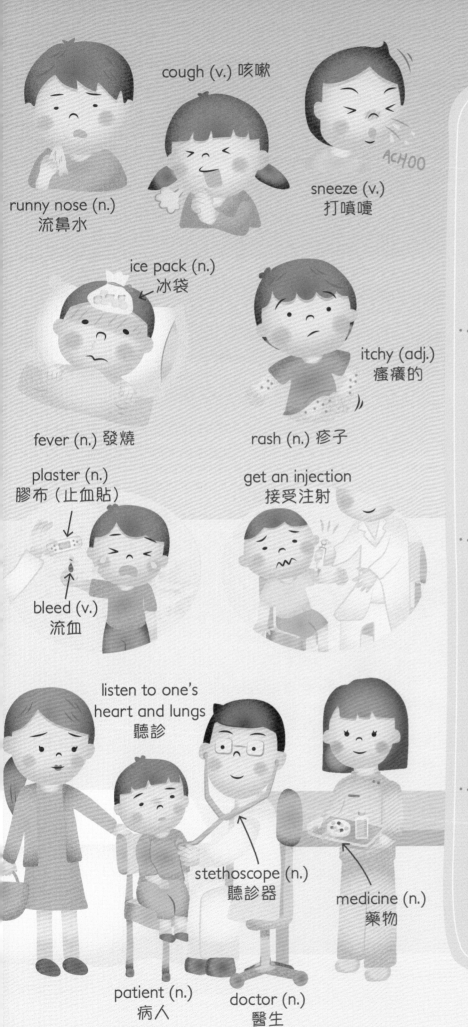

cough (v.) 咳嗽

sneeze (v.) 打噴嚏

runny nose (n.) 流鼻水

ice pack (n.) 冰袋

itchy (adj.) 瘙癢的

fever (n.) 發燒

rash (n.) 疹子

plaster (n.) 膠布（止血貼）

get an injection 接受注射

bleed (v.) 流血

listen to one's heart and lungs 聽診

stethoscope (n.) 聽診器

medicine (n.) 藥物

patient (n.) 病人

doctor (n.) 醫生

💬 Daily English

到診所看病時，我們應怎樣向醫生描述自己的病情呢？請説一説。

• I feel dizzy.
• I think I've got a fever.
• I've caught a cold.

❗ Rules to Know

醫護人員替我們治療時，需要使用一些工具，這時就要以 with 來表示。

• The receptionist took my temperature with a thermometer.
• The doctor listened to my heart with a stethoscope.

😆 Fun Corner

She was sick as a dog after eating street food. 不是指病得像狗一樣，而是表示吃了街邊小吃後吐得很厲害。

Hospital 醫院

ENG × 粵語   ENG × 普通話

inpatient (n.)
住院病人

call button (n.)
呼叫按鈕

visit (v.)
探望

screen (n.)
屏風

worried (adj.)
擔心

crutches (n.)
枴杖

on a drip 輸液

get well soon

medical
bed (n.)
病牀

---

operation theatre (n.) 手術室

X-ray (n.)
X 光片

surgeon (n.) 外科醫生

nurse (n.)
護士

mask (n.)
口罩

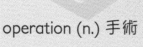
operation (n.) 手術

pharmacy (n.) 配藥處

white coat (n.)
白袍

ointment (n.)
藥膏

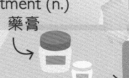

liquid medicine (n.)
藥水

pill (n.)
藥丸

54

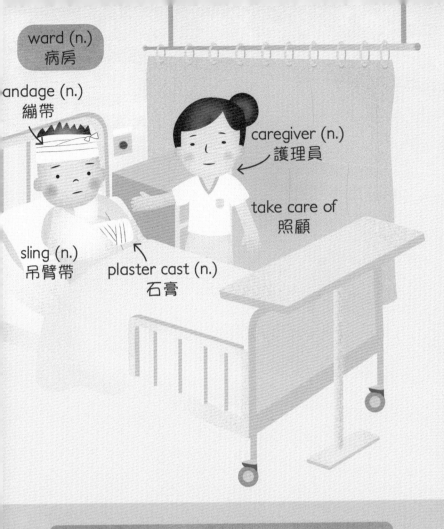

ward (n.)
病房

bandage (n.)
繃帶

caregiver (n.)
護理員

take care of
照顧

sling (n.)
吊臂帶

plaster cast (n.)
石膏

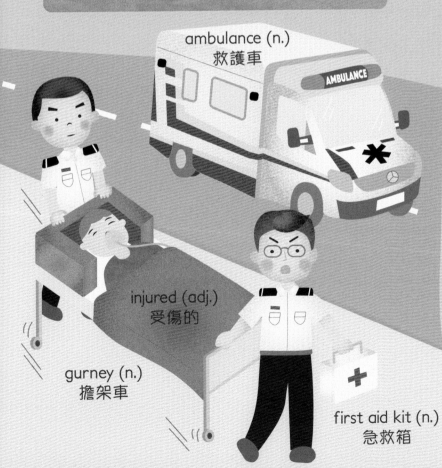

accident and emergency department (n.) ➡
急症室

ambulance (n.)
救護車

AMBULANCE

injured (adj.)
受傷的

gurney (n.)
擔架車

first aid kit (n.)
急救箱

😗 Let's Talk

Q: If you go to visit a patient in hospital, what will you bring?

A: I will bring some fruit.

Q: How should we behave in hospital?

A: We should keep our voice down in hospital.

💬 Daily English

如果要給住院的親友寫慰問卡，我們可以祝福對方早日康復！

• I hope you feel better soon.

• Wish you a speedy recovery.

⚠ Rules to Know

病人不能自行決定入院或出院，因此要用被動的方式來說明。

• Hannah was admitted to hospital.（被接收入院）

• She was discharged after the operation.（被允許出院）

😆 Fun Corner

看球賽時，如果出現 hospital pass（或稱 hospital ball）的話，就是指出現了容易令球員受傷的傳球。

55

Dental clinic
牙科診所

air and water jet (n.)
水氣噴槍

reflector (n.)
反光燈

mask (n.)
口罩

mouth
mirror (n.)
口腔鏡

medical gloves
(n.)
醫用手套

drill (n.)
牙鑽

dentist's
chair (n.)
牙醫診療椅

probe (n.)
牙探針

tooth transition (n.) 換牙

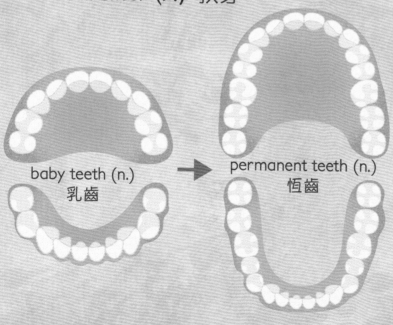

baby teeth (n.)
乳齒

permanent teeth (n.)
恆齒

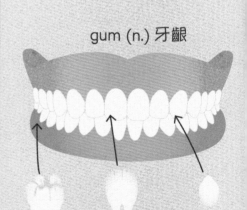

gum (n.) 牙齦

molar (n.)
臼齒

incisor (n.)
門齒

canine (n.)
犬齒

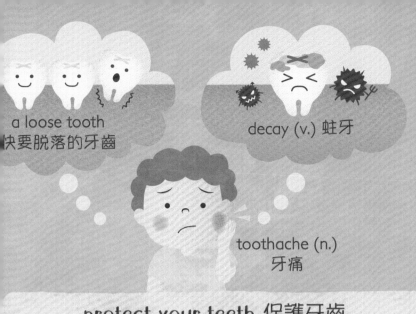

a loose tooth
快要脫落的牙齒

decay (v.) 蛀牙

toothache (n.)
牙痛

protect your teeth 保護牙齒

brush your teeth
刷牙

visit a dentist regularly
定期看牙醫

floss your teeth
用牙線清潔牙縫

eat less sugary foods
少吃甜食

Daily English

牙痛時，我們應怎樣向牙醫描述自己的情況呢？
- I have a toothache.
- I feel a pain in my teeth.

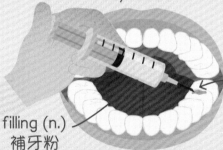

fill a cavity 補牙

cavity (n.)
蛀牙洞

filling (n.)
補牙粉

Rules to Know

你們每天刷牙多少次？每年看牙醫多少次？回答時可以用以下的方式：
- I brush my teeth twice a day.
  我每天刷牙兩次。
- I visit a dentist once a year.
  我每年看牙醫一次。

pull a tooth 拔牙

braces (n.)
牙箍（牙套）

Fun Corner

你們害怕拔牙嗎？Getting Paul to do exercise is like pulling teeth. 表示要 Paul 做運動就像拔牙一樣，真是一件很困難的事情呢！

Park 公園

playground (n.) 遊樂場

seesaw (n.) 蹺蹺板

climb (v.) 攀爬

slide down
滑下來

lawn (n.) 草地

bench (n.)
長椅

slide (n.) 滑梯

chase (v.)
追逐

swing (n.) 鞦韆

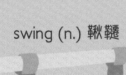

run (v.) 奔跑

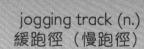

jogging track (n.)
緩跑徑（慢跑徑）

push (v.) 推

58

fence (n.) 籬笆

take a walk
散步

walk the dog 遛狗

lead (n.)
狗帶（狗繩）

hedge (n.)
樹籬

relaxed (adj.)
放鬆的

d the newspaper
看報紙

take a rest
休息

drinking fountain (n.)
飲水器

jog (v.) 慢跑

fountain (n.)
噴水池

sign (n.) 指示牌

KEEP OFF
THE GRASS

♪ Let's Talk

Q: What do you like to do in the park?

A: I like to play on the seesaw.

Q: How do you like playing on slides / swings?

A: It is so much fun.

💬 Daily English

我們應怎樣愛護公園裏的設施和環境呢？

- No littering.
  不准亂拋垃圾。
- Keep off the grass.
  不准踐踏草地。

⚠ Rules to Know

如果我們每天或每星期都會到公園去，這個習慣就要用簡單現在式來說明。注意人物不同，使用的動詞也會有變化啊！

- I go to the park every day.
- Sammy goes to the park every week.

😆 Fun Corner

當我們做一些輕而易舉的事情時，可以說 It's a walk in the park. 那就表示這件事就像到公園散步一般簡單呢！

Theme park 主題公園

cable car (n.) 纜車

cabin (n.) 乘客艙

That ...　This ...

Ferris wheel (n.) 摩天輪

fast (adj.) 飛快的

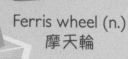

go-cart (n.) 小型賽車

booth (n.) 攤位

tent (n.) 帳篷

circus (n.) 馬戲團

clown (n.) 小丑

juggle (v.) 耍雜技

toss (v.) 拋

parade (n.) 巡遊

float (n.) 花車

60

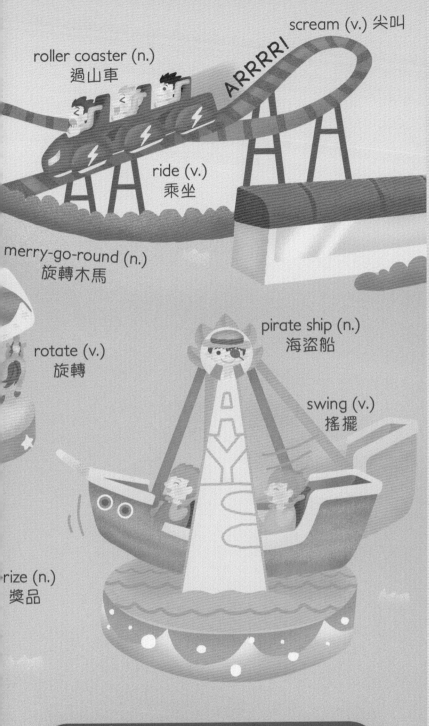

roller coaster (n.)
過山車

scream (v.) 尖叫

ARRRR!

ride (v.)
乘坐

merry-go-round (n.)
旋轉木馬

rotate (v.)
旋轉

pirate ship (n.)
海盜船

swing (v.)
搖擺

rize (n.)
獎品

firework display (n.)
煙花表演

castle (n.)
城堡

Let's Talk

Q: Which theme park have you visited?

A: I have visited Ocean Park.

Q: If you could choose a theme of a park, what would it be?

A: It would be about robots.

Daily English

主題公園給你怎樣的感覺呢？請用以下形容詞説一説。

- thrilling 驚險的
- exciting 刺激的
- crowded 擠迫的（擁擠的）

! Rules to Know

我們可用 this 提及附近的機動遊戲，用 that 提及遠處的機動遊戲，例如：

- This merry-go-round is lovely!
  這個旋轉木馬真漂亮！
- That Ferris wheel is huge!
  那個摩天輪真大！

Fun Corner

主題公園裏還有很多遊樂設施，令人樂而忘返！例如：drop tower（跳樓機）、haunted house（鬼屋）等。

Beach 沙灘

1

surfboard (n.) 滑浪板

surf (v.) 滑浪

lifeguard (n.) 救生員

lifeguard tower (n.) 救生員瞭望塔

paddle (v.) 用槳划船

wave (n.) 浪

kayak (n.) 獨木舟

snorkel (n.) 浮潛呼吸管

sunshade (n.) 太陽傘

sunglasses (n.) 太陽眼鏡

sunbathe (v.) 曬太陽

tan (n.) 古銅色皮膚

deckchair (n.) 沙灘椅

put on sunscreen 塗防曬乳

collect shells 拾貝殼

💬 Let's Talk

Q: How do you keep yourself safe on the beach?
A: I stay with my parents at all times.

Q: Besides sandcastles, what else can you make in the sand?
A: I think I can make a sand fish.

😆 Fun Corner

Surf 除了指滑浪外，還可用來表示上網，後面可搭配成 surf the Web 或 surf the Internet。

sail (n.)
帆

💬 Daily English

你們還記得沙灘的景色嗎？請說一說。
- The sea looks so clear.
  大海看上去很清澈。
- The sand is white and fine.
  沙又白又細。

! Rules to Know

在某些水上活動後面加上 ing，就能使動作變成名稱，例如：
- swim (v.)   → swimming (n.)
- windsurf (v.) → windsurfing (n.)

windsurf (v.)
玩滑浪風帆

choppy (adj.)
白浪滔滔的

swim (v.) 游泳

beach ball (n.)
沙灘球

sea (n.) 大海

sun hat (n.)
太陽帽

build a sandcastle
堆沙堡

spade (n.)
鏟子

seaside (n.)
海邊

sand (n.) 沙

 scoop (v.) 舀起

bucket (n.) 桶

63

Swimming pool
游泳池

coach (n)
教練

stretch (v.)
伸展

warm-up (n.) 熱身運動

swimming strokes 泳式

crawl (n.) 自由泳

breaststroke (n.) 蛙泳

butterfly (n.) 蝶泳

backstroke (n.) 背泳

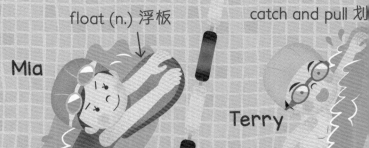

float (n.) 浮板

catch and pull 划

Mia

Terry

kick (v.) 踢水

hold the breath 憋氣

tread water 踩水

springboard (n.)
跳板

dive (v.) 跳水

splash (v.) 潑水

competition (n.)
比賽

trophy
(n.)
獎杯

🕑 Let's Talk

Q: What swimming aids do you use?

A: I use goggles.

Q: Do you like going to the pool or the beach?

A: I like going to the pool because the water is not salty.

😝 Fun Corner

My head swims. 當然不是指我的頭在游泳，而是頭暈呢！

⚠ Rules to Know

當我們比較游泳速度時，如果兩人游得一樣快，那就可以說 Mia swims as fast as Terry. 這種句式也可用來比較其他事情，例如：Crawl is as easy as breaststroke.

💬 Daily English

大家都希望在比賽中勝出，勝出後會得到什麼獎項呢？
• champion (n.) 冠軍
• runner-up (n.) 亞軍
• second runner-up (n.) 季軍

changing room (n.) 更衣室

lane (n.) 賽道

float (v.) 浮

sink (v.) 沉

goggles (n.)
泳鏡

swimsuit (n.)
泳衣

swim ring (n.)
泳圈

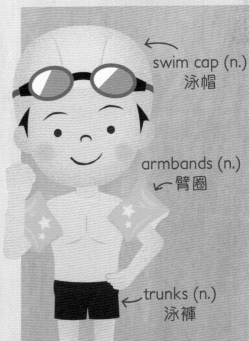

swim cap (n.)
泳帽

armbands (n.)
臂圈

trunks (n.)
泳褲

Library
圖書館

check-out 借書 / renewal 續借

I'd like to renew this book.
我想續借這本書。

library clerk (n.)
圖書館職員

library card (n.)
圖書證
（借書證）

check out a book
辦理借書手續

stack
the books
把書放好

pick (v.)
挑選

reading area (n.) 閱讀區

step stool
(n.)
腳踏凳

pop-up book (n.)
立體書

Bear Car

picture book (n.)
圖畫書

look for
尋找

librarian (n.)
圖書館管理員

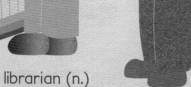

book drop box (n.) 還書箱

return (v.) 歸還

at's the due date?
哪一天是到期日？

pay an overdue fine
繳付過期罰款

lend (v.) 借出

borrow (v.) 借入

a pile of books
一疊書

book cover (n.) 封面

title (n.) 書名

author (n.) 作者

illustrator (n.) 插畫家

Happy Bear

By Elaine
Picture by HoiLam

read (v.) 閱讀

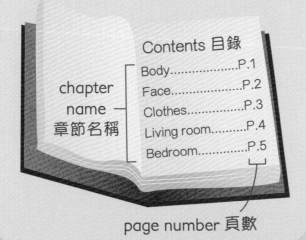

chapter name 章節名稱

Contents 目錄

Body....................P.1
Face.....................P.2
Clothes................P.3
Living room..........P.4
Bedroom..............P.5

page number 頁數

Let's Talk

Q: How many books do you read per month?

A: I read about five books per month.

Q: What was the last book you read?

A: The last book I read was a pop-up book.

Daily English

我們平日看的書上面會有一些重要資料，那是大家一定要認識的！例如：用 written by 或 story by，甚至簡單一個 by 來表示作者。而 illustrated by 或 picture by 則表示插畫家。

Rules to Know

當我們在文章寫出中文書名時，需要加上書名號，英文卻沒有這個標點符號。因此我們可以把英文書名改用斜體，或在書名下面畫線，即 *Happy Bear* 或 <u>Happy Bear</u>。

Fun Corner

我們會用「書蟲」來形容那些熱愛看書的人，英文中也有類似意思的字詞——bookworm。

Mall 商場

ENG × 粵語

ENG × 普通話

★ department store (n.) 百貨公司 ★

shop sign (n.)
商店招牌

the second floor 二樓

play area (n.)
兒童遊戲區

★ toy shop (n.) 玩具店 ★

the first floor 一樓

directory (n.)
商店指南

the ground floor
地下

customer services counter (n.)
顧客服務部

shop assistant (n.)
店員

May I help you?
有什麼可以幫你?

We're just looking.
我們只是看看。

sale (n.) 減價

SALE

elevator (n.) 升降機

customer (n.)
顧客

push the butto
按下按鈕

price tag (n.)
價錢牌

$639
expensive (adj.)
昂貴的

$20
cheap (adj.)
便宜的

electronic shop (n.) 電器店

furniture shop (n.) 家具店

shop (v.) 購物

fashion shop (n.) 時裝店

skating rink (n.) 溜冰場

ice-skate (v.) 溜冰

escalator (n.) 扶手電梯

hold the handrail 緊握扶手

stand still 站穩

Let's Talk

Q: When was the last time you went to a mall?

A: Last Sunday.

Q: Did you get anything?

A: Yes, Dad bought me a toy car.

Daily English

到商場購物時，我們可以怎樣請店員幫忙？

- I am looking for a gift for Mom. Where can I find...?
  我想給媽媽找一份禮物，在哪裏可以找到……？
- Would you please gift-wrap it for me?
  請問可以包裝成禮物嗎？

Rules to Know

說明商店在什麼樓層時，我們會用 on。

- The department store is on the second floor.
- The skating rink is on the ground floor.

Fun Corner

到商場不一定要買東西，光是逛逛也是賞心樂事，這種情況稱為 window shopping。

69

Arts and crafts 手工藝

paintbrush (n.) 畫筆

draw (v.) 用筆畫

palette (n.) 調色板

paint (v.) 用油彩畫

coloured pencil (n.) 木顏色（色鉛筆）

crayon (n.) 蠟筆

handicraft (n.) 手工藝

paste (v.) 貼

glue (n.) 漿糊（膠水）

cut (v.) 剪

scissors (n.) 剪刀

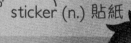

tape (n.) 膠帶

sticker (n.) 貼紙

mould (v.) 塑造

clay (n.) 黏土

sculpture (n.) 塑像

colours (n.) 顏色

red 紅色　　orange 橙色　　yellow 黃色　　green 綠色

blue 藍色　　purple 紫色　　pink 粉紅色　　brown 棕色

grey 灰色　　gold 金色　　silver 銀色　　black 黑色

shapes (n.) 形狀

circle (n.) 圓形

triangle (n.) 三角形

diamond (n.) 菱形

crescent (n.) 新月形

square (n.) 正方形

rectangle (n.) 長方形

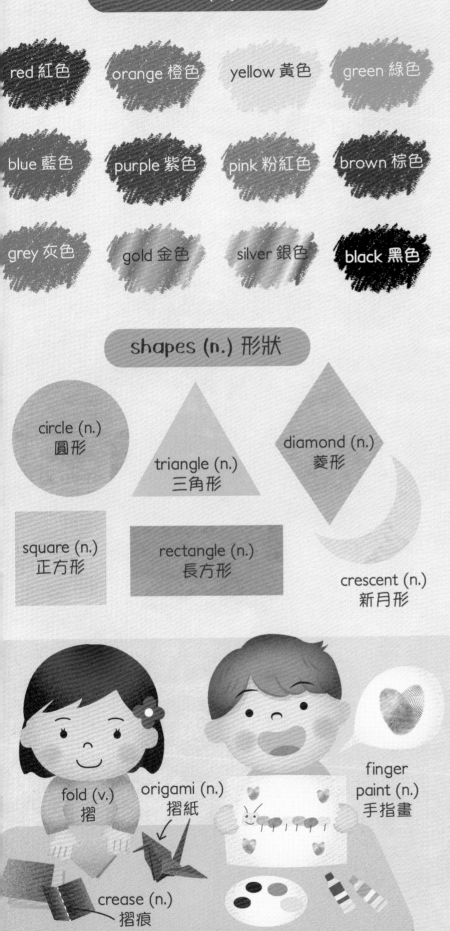

fold (v.) 摺

origami (n.) 摺紙

crease (n.) 摺痕

finger paint (n.) 手指畫

Daily English

製作手工藝，最重要的是什麼特質？請用以下句式説一説。

To make handicraft, you need to be...

• creative (adj.) 富創意的
• patient (adj.) 有耐性的

Rules to Know

顏色有不同的深淺，需要用不同的形容詞來表示，例如 reddish 的顏色比 red 淡一些。其他例子還有：

• yellowish　淺黃色的
• greenish　淺綠色的

Fun Corner

由我們親手製作的東西可以用 handmade 來形容，例如：This is a handmade card for my father.

HAPPY FATHER'S DAY

71

Music 音樂

classical music (n.) 古典音樂

orchestra (n.) 管弦樂團

flute (n.) 長笛

harp (n.) 豎琴

conductor (n.) 指揮

violin (n.) 小提琴

viola (n.) 中提琴

stage (n.) 舞台

band (n.) 樂隊

microphone (n.) 麥克風

guitar (n.) 結他（吉他）

keyboard (n.) 電子琴

dance (v.) 跳舞

drum set (n.) 爵士鼓

xylophone (n.) 木琴

musical notes (n.)
音符

trumpet (n.)
小號

sheet music (n.)
樂譜

music
stand (n.)
譜架

cello (n.)
大提琴

choir (n.)
合唱團

sing a song
唱歌

ano (n.) 鋼琴

musical instruments (n.) 樂器

recorder (n.)
豎笛 / 牧童笛

drum (n.)
鼓

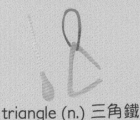

triangle (n.) 三角鐵

maracas (n.)
沙槌

tambourine (n.)
鈴鼓

Sports 運動

ENG × 粵語   ENG × 普通話

athletics 田徑運動

field (n.) 田賽

long jump (n.) 跳遠

high jump (n.) 跳高

shot put (n.) 推鉛球

discus (n.) 擲鐵餅

track (n.) 徑賽

start (v.) 起步

hurdles (n.) 跨欄

race (n.) 賽跑

finish (v.) 衝線

gymnastics (n.) 體操

the splits (n.) 分腿動作

judo (n.) 柔道

kung fu (n.) 功夫

cycling (n.) 騎單車 / 騎自行車

fencing (n.) 劍擊（擊劍）

Let's Talk

Q: What sport do you do regularly?
A: I play football every week.

Q: Why are sports important to us?
A: Because sports help us stay strong.

Daily English

看運動比賽時，人們會興高采烈地歡呼。大家試試用英文來歡呼吧！
• Wow!
• Bravo!
• Hurray!

ball games 球類運動

basketball (n.)
籃球

shoot (v.)
投球

score (n.) 分數

70 : 83

player (n.)
球員

lead (v.)
領先

football (n.)
足球

goal (n.) 球門

referee (n.) 裁判

pass (v.)
傳球

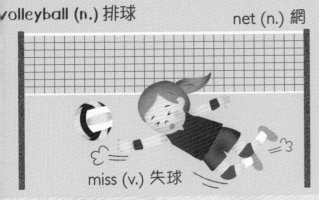

volleyball (n.) 排球

net (n.) 網

miss (v.) 失球

badminton (n.)
羽毛球

shuttlecock (n.)
羽毛球

hit (v.)
擊球

tennis (n.)
網球

racket (n.)
球拍

table tennis (n.)
乒乓球

bat (n.)
球拍

golf (n.)
高爾夫球

golf club (n.)
球杆

⚠ Rules to Know

我們做不同運動，會搭配不同的動詞，例如：
- play badminton / tennis / golf
- do fencing / gymnastics / judo

😆 Fun Corner

在美國，football 是指美式欖球，而不是我們熟知的足球。美國人會稱足球為 soccer，英國人則稱美式欖球為 American football，真混亂呢！

Playtime
遊戲時間

indoor games 室內遊戲

playmate (n.)
玩伴

throw the dice
擲骰子

think (v.)
思考

rock-paper-scissors (n.)
猜拳遊戲

build (v.) 搭建

building block (n.) 積木

outdoor games 戶外遊戲

tug of war (n.)
拔河

pull (v.) 拉

hopscotch (n.) 跳飛機（跳格子）

hop (v.)
單腳跳

ride (v.)
騎

scooter (n.) 踏板車

video game (n.)
電子遊戲

peek (v.)
偷看

hide-and-seek (n.)
捉迷藏

toys (n.) 玩具

robot (n.)
機械人（機器人）

doll (n.)
洋娃娃

teddy bear (n.)
玩具熊

toy train (n.)
玩具火車

jigsaw puzzle (n.)
拼圖遊戲

toy car (n.)
玩具車

spin (v.)
旋轉

top (n.) 陀螺

board games (n.)
桌上遊戲

chess piece (n.)
棋子

chess (n.) 國際象棋

Chinese chequers (n.)
波子棋（彈子跳棋）

Chinese chess (n.)
中國象棋

Let's Talk

Q: Who do you usually play games with?
A: I usually play games with my friends.
Q: Do you prefer indoor games or outdoor games?
A: I prefer outdoor games.

Daily English

跟別人玩遊戲時，我們會說什麼？
• Count me in! 我要一起玩！
• It's your turn. 輪到你了。
• I'll pass. 這一輪我不玩了。
• I won! 我勝出了！

Rules to Know

當我們說明自己兩個遊戲都不懂玩時，要用 or 來連接，例如：
I can't play top or chess.
如果兩個遊戲都懂玩，就可以說
I can play video games and chess.

Fun Corner

除了指遊戲外，game 還可以用來表示運動項目的比賽，例如：Dad enjoys watching basketball games.（爸爸喜歡看籃球比賽。）

Imaginary world
幻想世界

tiara (n.) 后冠

crown (n.) 王冠

castle (n.) 城堡

queen (n.) 王后／女王

king (n.) 國王

prince (n.) 王子　　princess (n.) 公主

fairy (n.) 小仙子

cast a spell 施咒語

magic (n.) 魔法

giant (n.) 巨人

dwarf (n.) 小矮人

wave the wand 揮動魔杖

witch (n.) 女巫

ghost (n.) 鬼→

vampire (n.) 吸血鬼

scary (adj.) 嚇人的

cemetery (n.) 墓地

zombie (n.) 喪屍

dragon (n.)
龍

phoenix (n.)
鳳凰

alien (n.)
外星人

unicorn (n.) 獨角獸

UFO (n.)
不明飛行物體

protect (v.)
保護

sword (n.)
劍 →

eyepatch (n.)
眼罩

mermaid (n.)
人魚

treasure (n.)
寶藏

pirate (n.)
海盜

knight (n.) 騎士

superhero (n.) 超級英雄

VS

villain (n.) 壞人

WIN
(v.)
勝利

LOSE
(v.)
落敗

cape (n.)
披肩

Let's Talk

Q: Do you like fairy tales? Why?

A: Yes, I do. I like fairy tales because they are adventurous.

Q: What imaginary character would you like to be?

A: I would like to be a knight.

Daily English

你們心目中的幻想世界是怎樣的呢？請參考以下形容詞說一說。
• mysterious 神秘的
• fantastic 美妙的
• frightening 可怕的
• romantic 浪漫的

Rules to Know

這些幻想故事一般是在從前發生的事情，因此說故事時往往會使用簡單過去式。例如：Once upon a time, there was a beautiful castle.（很久以前，有一座漂亮的城堡。）

Fun Corner

Dragon 是西方幻想故事裏的生物，是邪惡的化身。中國的龍譯作英文也是 dragon，但牠卻是吉祥的象徵。

Jobs
職業

 ENG × 粵語   ENG × 普通話

police officer (n.)
警察

postman (n.)
郵差（郵遞員）

nurse (n.)
護士

doctor (n.)
醫生

🗣 Let's Talk

Q: What is your dream job? / What do you want to be when you grow up?

A: My dream job is to be a bus driver. / I want to be a teacher when I grow up.

💬 Daily English

如果想知道別人的職業是什麼，我們可以這樣問：

- What's your job?
- What do you do?

painter (n.)
油漆工

painter (n.)
畫家

actor / actress (n.)
演員

magician (n.)
魔術師

⚠ Rules to Know

有些以 er 結尾的單詞是來自動詞，指做這個動作的人，例如：

- teach (v.) 教導
  → teacher (n.) 教師
- write (v.) 寫作
  → writer (n.) 作家

astronaut (n.)
太空人（宇航員）

writer (n.)
作家

architect (n.)
建築師

builder (n.)
建築工人

😆 Fun Corner

A good job 當然是指一份好工作，但在英文中常説的 Good job! 其實是稱讚別人做得好呢！

firefighter (n.)
消防員

makeup artist (n.)
化妝師

hairdresser (n.)
理髮師

chef (n.)
廚師

dentist (n.)
牙醫

lawyer (n.)
律師

judge (n.)
法官

musician (n.)
音樂家

singer (n.)
歌手

dancer (n.)
舞蹈員

pilot (n.)
飛機師

flight
attendant (n.)
空中服務員

farmer (n.)
農夫

fisherman (n.)
漁夫

photographer (n.)
攝影師

camera (n.)
相機

reporter (n.)
記者

electrician (n.)
電工

plumber (n.)
水管工

animal trainer (n.)
動物訓練員

veterinarian (n.)
獸醫

shion designer (n.)
時裝設計師

scientist (n.)
科學家

athlete (n.)
運動員

student (n.)
學生

teacher (n.)
教師

Every job is
important!
每種職業都很重要!

81

Transportation
交通工具

container ship (n.)
貨櫃船（貨船）

helicopter (n.)
直升機

pier (n.) 碼頭

ferry (n.) 渡輪

boat (n.)
小船

traffic sign (n.)
交通標誌

bicycle (n.)
單車（自行車）

traffic jam (n.)
交通擠塞（交通堵塞）

taxi (n.) 的士

car (n.) 汽車

minibus (n.) 小巴

lorry (n.)
貨車

coach (n.) 旅遊巴

traffic light (n.) 交通信號燈

pedestrian light 行人過路燈

flash (v.)
閃動

car crash (n.) 車禍

'red man' light (n.)
紅燈

'green man' light (n.)
綠燈

ship (n.) 輪船

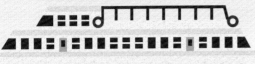

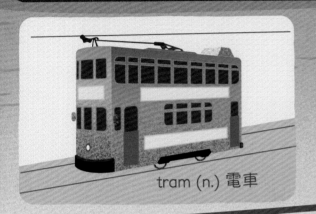

tram (n.) 電車

yellow
flashing
beacon
黃色閃燈

look all around
環顧四周

motorcycle (n.)
電單車（摩托車）

school bus (n.)
校車

jaywalk (v.)
胡亂過馬路

traffic
island (n.)
安全島

cross the road 過馬路

zebra crossing (n.)
斑馬線

👄 Let's Talk

Q: What should you do when you cross the road?

A: I should wait for the 'green man' light.

Q: Do you cross the road on your own?

A: No. I always cross the road with my parents.

💬 Daily English

提醒路人注意交通時，可用以下表示「小心！」的句子：
- Watch out!
- Be careful!

❗ Rules to Know

我們會用 by 來表示乘搭什麼交通工具到某個地方去，例如：
- I go to school by minibus.

如果是走路的，就會這樣說：
- Mom goes to work on foot.

😆 Fun Corner

不少交通工具上都設有安全帶。用英文請別人繫好安全帶叫 Buckle your seatbelt up. 或簡單得連「安全帶」也省略掉，說 Buckle up.

Take the bus 乘搭巴士

ENG × 粵語　ENG × 普通話

single deck bus (n.) 單層巴士

bus stop sign (n.) 巴士站牌

15A　16　13M　落客站　BUS

upper deck (n.) 上層

destination (n.) 目的地

route number (n.) 路線編號

旺角 MONG KOK 16

lower deck (n.) 下層

wheelchair ramp 輪椅斜板

double deck bus (n.) 雙層巴士

catch the bus 追趕巴士

bus driver (n.) 巴士司機

drive (v.) 駕駛

stairway (n.) 樓梯

card reader (n.) 讀卡器

$5.2
$2.6

pay the fare 付車資

sit (v.) 坐下

tap the card 拍卡

84

bus shelter (n.)
巴士候車亭

get on 上車

get off 下車

hold the handrail
緊握扶手

press the bell
按鈴

seat (n.)
座位

block the doorway
阻擋出入口

Let's Talk

Q: Do you prefer the upper deck or lower deck on a bus?

A: I prefer the upper deck.

Q: How often do you take the bus?

A: I take the bus once a week to visit my grandmother.

Daily English

乘搭巴士時，如果遇到困難，應怎樣向司機查詢呢？

• Does this bus go to Cultural Centre?
這輛巴士去文化中心嗎？

• Where should we get off?
我們應在哪裏下車？

Rules to Know

當我們提及在巴士上發生的事情時，會用 on the bus 來說明，例如：

• He slept on the bus.

• We should not run on the bus.

Fun Corner

bus station 和 bus stop 有什麼分別呢？其實 station 指巴士總站，可以停泊多輛巴士。而 stop 則是中途站，佔用的空間比 station 小得多。

Take the train 乘搭鐵路

concourse (n.) 大堂

one-way ticket (n.)
單程票

top up
增值（充值）

ticket machine (n.)   售票機

route map (n.)
路線圖

buy a ticket
買票

entrance gate (n.)
入閘口

exit gate (n.)
出閘口

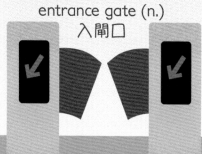

turnstile (n.)
旋轉閘門

carriage (n.) 車廂

disabled (adj.)
殘疾的

passenger (n.)
乘客

elderly (adj.) 年老的

gap (n.)
空隙

depart (v.) 離開

Bye!

rail (n.) 路軌

arrive (v.) 到達

platform gate (n.)
月台閘門

platform (n.) 月台

strap hanger (n.)
扶手吊帶

priority seat
優先座

give up one's seat
讓座

pregnant (adj.) 懷孕的

💬 Daily English

乘搭鐵路時有很多規則要注意，大家有沒有好好遵守這些規則呢？

• Do not lean against the pole.
切勿靠在扶手柱上。

• Do not rush onto the train.
切勿衝門。

⚠ Rules to Know

當我們比較火車和汽車這兩種事物時，就可以使用 than，例如：

• A train is faster than a car.
火車的速度比汽車快。

• A car is smaller than a train.
汽車比火車小。

😆 Fun Corner

你乘搭過以下鐵路系統的交通工具嗎？

• 地下鐵路：subway / metro / underground

• 高速鐵路：high-speed train

• 地面的輕軌鐵路：light railway

Take the plane 乘搭飛機

take off 起飛

land (v.) 降落

check-in counter (n.)
登機櫃枱

boarding pass (n.)
登機證

security checkpoint (n.)
保安檢查閘口

metal detector (n.)
金屬探測器

X-ray machine (n.)
Ⅹ光機

flight attendant (n.)
空中服務員

overhead locker (n.)
上方的行李櫃

Excuse me!

window seat (n.)
靠窗座位

←aisle seat (n.)→
靠走廊座位

board a plane 登機

tray table (n.)
餐桌

in-flight meal (n.)
飛機餐

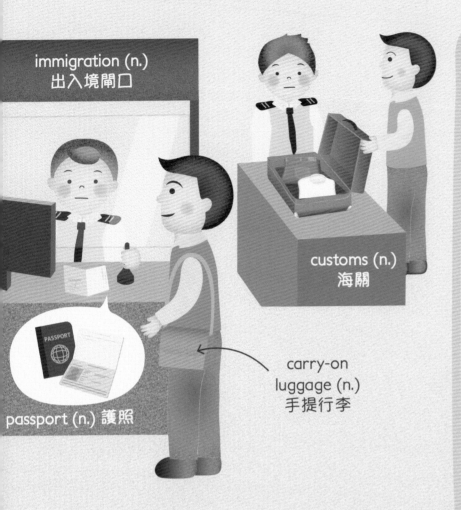

immigration (n.)
出入境閘口

customs (n.)
海關

passport (n.) 護照

carry-on luggage (n.)
手提行李

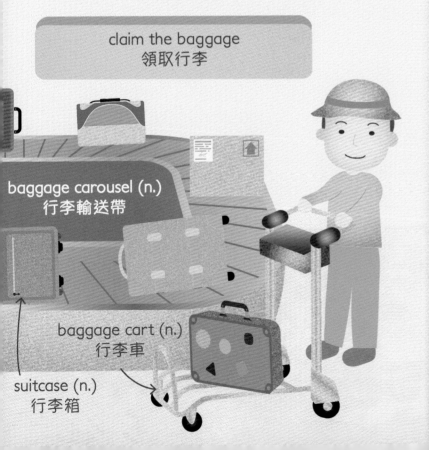

claim the baggage
領取行李

baggage carousel (n.)
行李輸送帶

baggage cart (n.)
行李車

suitcase (n.)
行李箱

Let's Talk

Q: Have you ever taken a plane? Where did you go?

A: Yes, I have. I took a plane to Japan last summer.

Q: Do you like to travel by plane? Why?

A: Yes, I do. Because I can see clouds.

Daily English

在飛機上，我們常常需要空中服務員協助。在提出要求時加上 Excuse me，會顯得更有禮貌啊！例如：Excuse me, may I have a blanket?（打擾一下，請問我可以要一條毛毯嗎？）

Rules to Know

登機前有很多事情要做，要怎樣才可有條理地表達次序？

1. First, check in at the check-in counter.
2. Next, go through security.
3. Last, go through immigration.

Fun Corner

飛機 plane 的英式英文又稱為 aeroplane，而美式英文則叫 airplane。

Town 市區

ENG × 粵語   ENG × 普通話

park (n.) 公園

footbridge (n.) 行人天橋

pedestrian (n.) 行人

pharmacy (n.) 藥房

coffee shop (n.) 咖啡店

corner (n.) 街角

mall (n.) 商場

canal (n.) 運河

car park (n.) 停車場

ancient (adj.) 古老的

cinema (n.) 電影院

ice cream van (n.) 雪糕車

bookshop (n.) 書店

pavement (n.) 行人道

church (n.) 教堂

post office (n.) 郵政局

mailbox (n.) 郵箱

bank (n.) 銀行

How do I get to the bookshop?

post (v.) 郵寄

streetlight (n.) 街燈（路燈）

petrol station (n.) 加油站

90

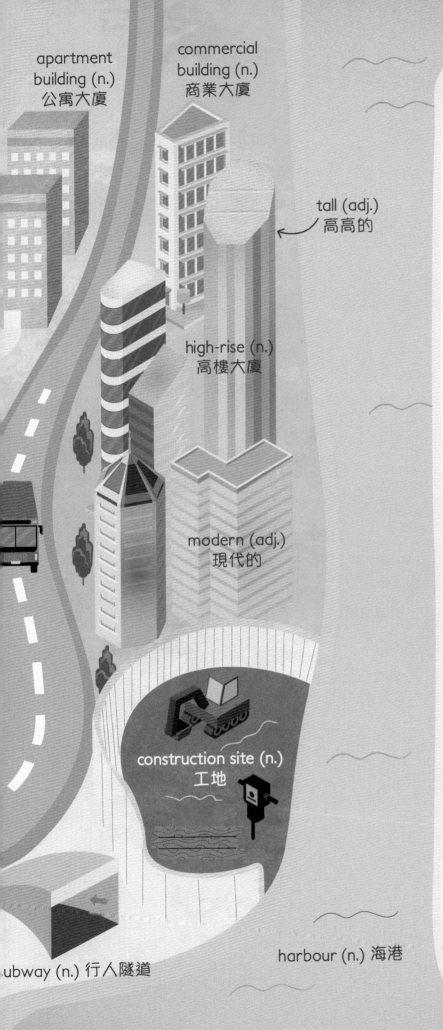

apartment building (n.)
公寓大廈

commercial building (n.)
商業大廈

tall (adj.)
高高的

high-rise (n.)
高樓大廈

modern (adj.)
現代的

construction site (n.)
工地

ubway (n.) 行人隧道

harbour (n.) 海港

Let's Talk

Q: Where is the cinema?

A: The cinema is near the mall.

Q: Where would you like to visit in town?

A: I would like to visit a church.

Daily English

在城市裏常常碰到有人問路，這時我們應怎樣指示正確的方向？

1. Go straight ahead.
   向前走。
2. And then turn right.
   然後往右轉。
3. The bookshop is on your left.
   書店就在你左邊。

⚠ Rules to Know

你找到這個城市裏最高的建築物嗎？表達「最高」的時候，我們會用 the tallest。一起看看其他例子！

• the cleanest city
  最清潔的城市
• the biggest park
  最大的公園

Fun Corner

「街道」分成很多種類，在香港常見的有 street（街）、road（路／道）、lane（里）、path（徑）等。

People around the world
世界各地的人

wave the flag 揮旗

Japanese 日本人

Korean 韓國人

Chinese 中國人

Filipino 菲律賓人

wave (v.) 揮手

national flag 國旗

Russian 俄羅斯人

the French 法國人

shake hands 握手

Italian 意大利人

friend (n.) 朋友

Mexican 墨西哥人

American 美國人

Indonesian 印尼人

Let's Talk

Q: Do you have any foreign friends? Where are they from?

A: Yes, I do. They are from Australia.

Q: How many stars are there on the flag of China?

A: There are five stars.

Fun Corner

認識世界各地的人,能夠拓闊我們的眼光。在英文中,就可用 eye-opener 來指令人大開眼界的事物。

Vietnamese 越南人

Indian 印度人

Thai 泰國人

British 英國人

the Dutch 荷蘭人

German 德國人

Australian 澳洲人

greet (v.) 問候

Hello!
你好！

Canadian 加拿大人

Spanish 西班牙人

💬 Daily English

認識新朋友時，你們會怎樣介紹自己呢？
• 名字：I am Ken.
• 地方：I am from Hong Kong, China.
• 年齡：I am seven years old.
• 打招呼：It's nice to meet you.

❗ Rules to Know

有些指人民的字詞還可以表示那個地方使用的語言，或形容來自當地的事物，例如：
• Do you speak Japanese?（語言）
• I love Japanese food.（當地事物）

Landmarks
世界名勝

Elizabeth Tow●
伊利沙伯塔

Statue of Liberty
自由女神像

North America
北美洲

The United
Kingdom 英國

Grand Canyon
大峽谷

The United States of
America 美國

Christ the Redeemer
救世基督像

Pacific Ocean
太平洋

It's such a wonderful world!
世界真美好呢！

adventure (n.)
冒險

Brazil
巴西

South America
南美洲

Atlantic Ocea●
大西洋

Moai
復活節島石像

Chile 智利

🗣 Let's Talk

Q: Which country would you like to visit?

A: I would like to visit France.

Q: What landmark would you create for your neighbourhood?

A: I would create a big statue.

💬 Daily English

有很多名勝都是歷史建築，我們可以用以下形容詞來描述：
- historic 有歷史意義的
- famous 著名的
- grand 宏偉的

94

Arctic Ocean
北冰洋

Saint Basil's Cathedral
聖瓦西里主教座堂

Russia 俄羅斯

Forbidden City
故宮

China 中國

Mount Fuji
富士山

Japan 日本

Europe 歐洲

Colosseum
羅馬鬥獸場

Asia 亞洲

Italy 意大利

Merlion Statue
魚尾獅雕像

Africa 非洲

The Great Sphinx of Giza
獅身人面像

Singapore 新加坡

Egypt 埃及

Sydney
Opera House
悉尼歌劇院

Indian Ocean
印度洋

Australia 澳洲

Oceania
大洋洲

map (n.) 地圖

Antarctica 南極洲

Weather and seasons

spring (n.) 春天

cloud (n.) 雲

summer (n.) 夏天

rainbow (n.) 彩虹

umbrella (n.) 雨傘

sweat (n.) 汗水
(v.) 流汗

wet (adj.) 濕淋淋的

puddle (n.) 水窪

rain (n.) 雨
(v.) 下雨

winter (n.) 冬天

snow (n.) 雪
(v.) 下雪

autumn (n.) 秋天

ice (n.) 冰

frost (n.) 霜

freeze (v.) 結冰

snowman (n.) 雪人

cold (adj.) 寒冷的

weather forecast 天氣預報

sunny (adj.) 天晴的

partly cloudy 局部多雲的

rainy (adj.) 下雨的

stormy (adj.) 有雷暴的

天氣和季節

ENG × 粵語　ENG × 普通話

sunshine (n.) 陽光

sun (n.) 太陽

hot (adj.) 炎熱的

shade (n.) 陰涼處

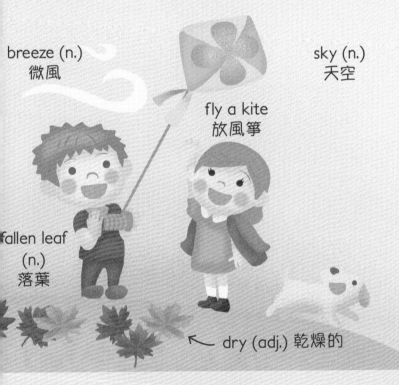

breeze (n.) 微風

sky (n.) 天空

fly a kite 放風箏

fallen leaf (n.) 落葉

dry (adj.) 乾燥的

windy (adj.) 大風的

cloudy (adj.) 多雲的

foggy (adj.) 有霧的

💬 Let's Talk

Q: What is your favourite season? Why?

A: My favourite season is summer because I love sunbathing.

Q: What do you like doing in autumn?

A: I like having a picnic in autumn.

💬 Daily English

今天的天氣怎麼樣？請大家說一說。
- It's 25°C (degrees Celsius).
- It's a lovely day, isn't it?
- The weather is terrible today.

❗ Rules to Know

在一些天氣現象的名詞後面加上 y，可以變成形容詞。
- rain ⟶ rainy
- wind ⟶ windy
- cloud ⟶ cloudy

😆 Fun Corner

不同形式的雨有不同叫法，例如：
- drizzle (n.) 毛毛細雨
- shower (n.) 驟雨
- downpour (n.) 短暫暴雨

我們還可以說 It's raining cats and dogs. 來形容傾盆大雨。

Nature
大自然

ENG × 粵語

ENG × 普通話

the Northern lights (n.)
北極光

iceberg (n.) 冰山

erupt (v.)
爆發

lava (n.)
熔岩

volcano (n.) 火山

jungle (n.)
叢林

desert (n.)
沙漠

cliff (n.)
懸崖

waterfall (n.)
瀑布

peak (n.)
山頂

mountain (n.)
高山

valley (n.) 山谷

hill (n.) 小山

lake (n.) 湖泊

river (n.) 河流

flow (v.) 流動

natural disasters 自然災害

earthquake (n.) 地震

typhoon (n.) 颱風

tornado (n.) 龍捲風

flood (n.) 洪水

drought (n.) 旱災

wildfire (n.) 山火

tsunami (n.) 海嘯

damage (n.) 破壞

🗣 Let's Talk

Q: Are there any beautiful natural landscapes in Hong Kong?

A: Yes, there are waterfalls and hills in Hong Kong.

Q: How can we help the people affected by natural disasters?

A: We can donate money to them.

💬 Daily English

大自然的力量驚人，以下形容詞就可以用來描述自然災害的破壞：
- huge 巨大的
- serious 嚴重的
- tragic 悲慘的

⚠ Rules to Know

我們可用 often 來説明經常發生的事情，例如：Wildfires often occur during dry periods.（乾燥的日子經常會發生山火。）

😆 Fun Corner

有時會在新聞上聽到 hurricane 颶風這個字詞，它跟 typhoon 颱風其實是相同的自然現象，只是在不同地點發生，而香港就只會颳颱風！

Save the earth 保護地球

ENG × 粵語　ENG × 普通話

water pollution 水污染

poisonous (adj.) 有毒的

soil pollution 土地污染

landfill (n.) 垃圾堆填區

electronic waste (n.) 電子廢物

air pollution 空氣污染

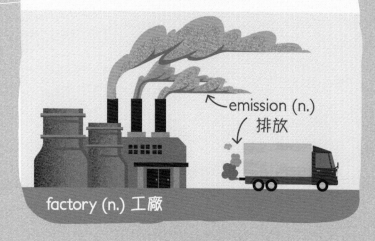

emission (n.) 排放

factory (n.) 工廠

renewable energy (n.) 可再生能源

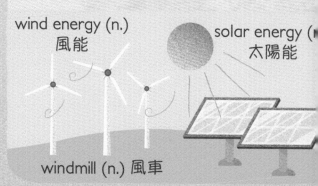

wind energy (n.) 風能

solar energy (n.) 太陽能

windmill (n.) 風車

plant a tree 植樹

refuse (v.) 拒絕

bring your own bag 自備購物袋

🗣 Let's Talk

Q: What makes the earth sick?
A: There is too much rubbish.

Q: How can you reduce waste?
A: I can use less tissues.

💬 Daily English

我們應怎樣在日常生活中保護環境?

• No straw, please.
　不要飲管（吸管），謝謝。

• I don't need the plastic bag, thanks.
　我不要膠袋（塑料袋），謝謝。

recycle 循環再造

recycling bin (n.) 回收箱

sort (v.) 分類

cardboard (n.) 硬紙板

waste (n.) 廢物

glass (n.) 玻璃

paper (n.) 紙張

metal (n.) 金屬

plastic (n.) 塑料

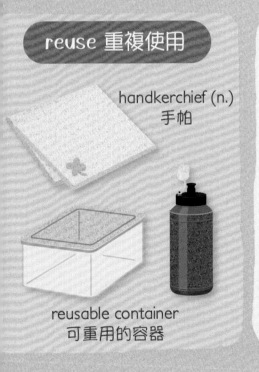

reuse 重複使用

handkerchief (n.) 手帕

reusable container 可重用的容器

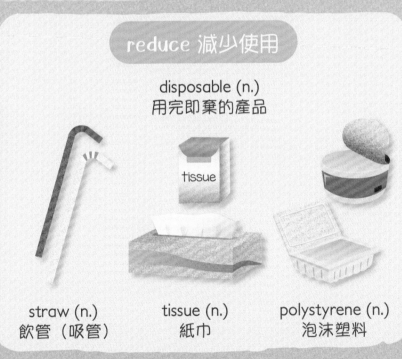

reduce 減少使用

disposable (n.) 用完即棄的產品

tissue

straw (n.) 飲管（吸管）

tissue (n.) 紙巾

polystyrene (n.) 泡沫塑料

(!) **Rules to Know**

use（使用）這個動詞可以變身成不同的詞語，表達相關的意思：
- reuse (v.) 重複使用　　used (adj.) 用過的
- useless (adj.) 沒用的　　useful (adj.) 有用的

(≧) **Fun Corner**

植物對環境非常重要，因此代表植物的顏色 green 也成了跟環保息息相關的詞語，例如：It's easy to go green.（保護環境是很容易的事。）

Space
太空

ENG × 粵語 ENG × 普通話

the solar system (n.) 太陽系

universe (n.) 宇宙

Moon (n.) 月球

Mars (n.) 火星

Venus (n.) 金星

Jupiter (n.) 木星

Sun (n.) 太陽

Earth (n.) 地球

Mercury (n.) 水星

weightless (adj.) 無重的

spacesuit (n.) 太空衣

space shuttle (n.) 太空穿梭機（航天飛機）

astronaut (n.) 太空人（宇航員）

Let's Talk

Q: If you could travel around the universe, what would you bring along?

A: I would bring along my favourite snacks.

Q: What does an astronaut do?

A: An astronaut performs tasks in space.

Daily English

我們可以怎樣表達對宇宙的好奇心呢？

- I wonder how big the universe is.
  我想知道宇宙有多大。

- I am interested in other planets.
  我對其他行星感興趣。

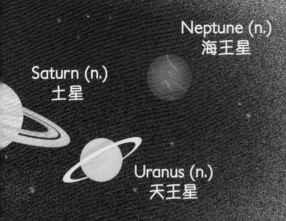

Saturn (n.)
土星

Neptune (n.)
海王星

Uranus (n.)
天王星

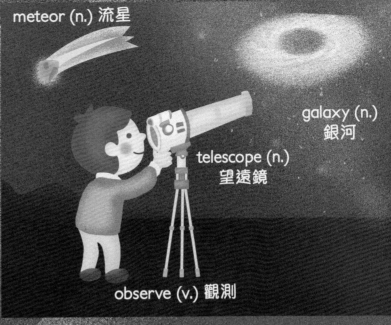

meteor (n.) 流星

galaxy (n.)
銀河

telescope (n.)
望遠鏡

observe (v.) 觀測

satellite (n.)
人造衞星

black hole (n.)
黑洞

orbit (n.) 軌道

revolve (v.)
旋轉

solar eclipse (n.) 日蝕
lunar eclipse (n.) 月蝕

rocket (n.)
火箭

launch (v.)
發射

set foot on a planet
踏足行星

B612

⚠ Rules to Know

我們可用 How 來問關於太空的問題，例如：

• How far is the Sun from the Earth?
太陽距離地球有多遠？

• How big is the Moon?
月球有多大？

😆 Fun Corner

跟火箭有關的科學是不是很艱深呢？
因此 It's not rocket science. 這句
話常常用來比喻事情不算很困難。

Prepositions 介詞

position 位置

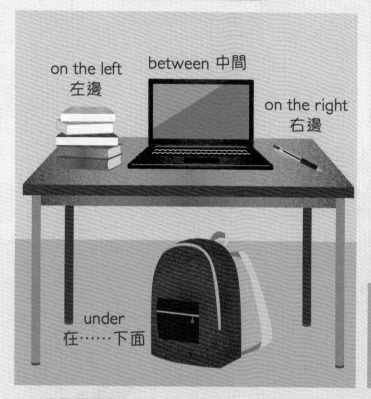

on the left 左邊

between 中間

on the right 右邊

under 在……下面

above 在上方

I am above the house.
我在屋子上方。

on 在……上面

behind 後面

in 裏面

besides / next to 旁邊

in front of 前面

movement 動作

I am jumping onto the box.
我跳到盒子上面。

onto 到……上面

over 越過

through 穿過

off 從……下來

into 到……入面

out of 從……出來

I am walking across the road.
我橫過馬路。

across 橫過

around 圍繞

up 向上

down 向下

Opposite 相反詞

big 大　small 小

hard 硬

soft 軟

clean 乾淨
dirty 骯髒

fast 快
slow 慢

thick 厚　thin 薄

bright 光（亮）
dark 暗

fat 胖　thin 瘦

far 遠
near 近

The water is shallow here.
The water is deep here.

long 長
short 短

light 輕
heavy 重

shallow 淺
deep 深

The soup is hot.
The juice is cold.

hot 熱

cold 冷

noisy 吵鬧　quiet 安靜

old 年老　young 年輕

1 + 1 = 2　365 + 789
2 + 2 = 4　= 1053 ✗
3 + 3 = 6　642 + 756
4 + 4 = 8　= 1399 ✗
5 + 5 = 10　319 + 232
6 + 6 = 12　= 561 ✗
correct 正確　wrong 錯誤

tall 高
short 矮

wide 闊（寬）

narrow 窄

open 開

closed 關

full 滿　empty 空

high 高
low 低

old 舊　new 新

Answer a question 答問題

請在橫線上加上適當的內容，回答以下問題。你可以參考括號內的提示和建議的答案，幫助思考。

Question 1 What do you usually do at weekends?

I usually _____ at weekends.

go to the beach

do shopping with Mom

play games with friends

Question 2 Can you tell me about yourself?

I am ____(your name)____. I am ____(your age)____ years old. I like _____.

swimming

reading

drawing

Question 3 Can you tell me about your parents?

My father / mother is _____.

a doctor

an architect

a flight attendant

a writer

He / She is ____(tall / short / big / small)____.

He / She _____ with me every week.

plays football

plays video games

Make a sentence 造句子

請根據圖畫和括號內的提示，在橫線填上適當的英文字詞，使句子的意思完整。然後扮演圖中的角色，把對話說出來。

1 Am I too _____ (adj.) ?

2 I can _____ (v.) the floor.

3 I'm really _____ (adj.) !

4 The flowers _____ (v.) so good !

5 I travel around the space by _____ (n.).

6 I hide _____ (prep.) the tree.

7 I _____ (v.) the paper with _____ (n.).

8 I want to _____ (v.) a _____ (n.).

Mixed-up story 故事排序

請根據圖畫和描述文字，重新排列成一個完整的故事，把數字 1 - 4 填在方格內，然後把故事順序說出來。

1

The ambulancemen sent him to hospital.

3

He hurt his arm and his head. He looked very sad.

2

So I gave him a card and some chocolate. I hope he can get well soon.

4

Last Sunday, my brother had a car crash.

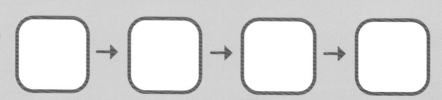

What's the order?

☐ → ☐ → ☐ → ☐

參考答案：4、1、3、2

What do they say? 他們說什麼？

請根據圖畫內容，選出適當的對話。然後扮演故事中的角色，把對話說出來。

1. A. Hi, I'm a robber.
   B. Give me your bag!

2. A. Can you help me catch the robber, please?
   B. There was a robbery reported on Happy Street.

3. A. Don't move!
   B. I have a truncheon.

4. A. You are arrested.
   B. Do you like the handcuffs?

5. A. Salute!
   B. This is my police dog.

Wonderful story! 奇妙的故事！

請選出你喜歡的內容，創作一個屬於你的故事。你也可發揮創意，構思有趣的情節！

When?

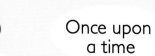

Last Monday

Yesterday

Once upon a time

Last summer

Who?

a witch

a superhero

a dragon

a zombie

Where?

desert

jungle

castle

cemetery

park

What?

started an adventure

survived a tornado

found treasure

met a ghost

How does the character feel?

surprised

annoyed

angry

excited

In the end?

rode on a rocket

turned into a sculpture

had a party

作者簡介

Elaine Tin 田依莉

持有翻譯及傳譯榮譽文學學士學位和語文學碩士學位，曾任兒童圖書翻譯及編輯。熱愛英文教學，喜與兒童互動，故於二零一四年成為英文導師，把知識、經驗和興趣結合起來，讓學生愉快地學習。她認為每個孩子都是獨特的，如能在身旁陪伴和輔助，就能激發他們的興趣和潛質。

LEARN and USE English in Context

活學活用英文詞彙大圖典（修訂版）

作　　　者：Elaine Tin
繪　　　圖：HoiLam、歐偉澄
責任編輯：林沛暘、潘曉華
美術設計：陳雅琳、劉麗萍
出　　　版：新雅文化事業有限公司
　　　　　　香港英皇道499號北角工業大廈18樓
　　　　　　電話：(852) 2138 7998
　　　　　　傳真：(852) 2597 4003
　　　　　　網址：http://www.sunya.com.hk
　　　　　　電郵：marketing@sunya.com.hk
發　　　行：香港聯合書刊物流有限公司
　　　　　　香港荃灣德士古道220-248號荃灣工業中心16樓
　　　　　　電話：(852) 2150 2100
　　　　　　傳真：(852) 2407 3062
　　　　　　電郵：info@suplogistics.com.hk
印　　　刷：中華商務彩色印刷有限公司
　　　　　　香港新界大埔汀麗路36號
版　　　次：二〇二二年九月初版
　　　　　　二〇二四年八月第三次印刷

ISBN: 978-962-08-8094-0